Into the Ruins

Fall 2019

Issue 14

COPYRIGHT

Published September 2019 by Figuration Press
Portland, Oregon

Into the Ruins is a project and publication of Figuration Press,
a small publication house focused on alternate visions of the future
and alternate ways of understanding the world,
particularly in ecological contexts.

intotheruins.com

figurationpress.com

ISBN 13: 978-1-950213-01-6
ISBN 10: 1-950213-01-3

Editor's Note:
Getting back on track. One hopes.
We'll see if I have to change this before release.

Comments and feedback always welcome at editor@intotheruins.com
Comments for authors will be forwarded.

Issue 14
Fall 2019

TABLE OF CONTENTS

PREAMBLE

GROWING STILL

BY JOEL CARIS

WE KEPT MEANING TO DO IT ON A SATURDAY MORNING. Take our mugs of coffee and our books and sit on the back patio, out in the sun now that summer really had arrived. It was mostly Kate who kept mentioning it, just never on a Saturday morning. Then we would forget. Or we would remember, but it was raining that morning. This Northwest summer has been more like the ones I remember from my youth, stretches of progressively hotter days broken by cooler, overcast, and even rainy ones. Oddly, after so many years of warmer, drier summers, it has felt strange and out of place.

The window for this is small. Sunday mornings are less leisurely, as our regular farmers market takes place then and so we tend to cut short our coffee and books time, get moving both to get the most out of the day and not miss the more limited types of produce—especially now, as the corn and melons are coming on. Otherwise, we work a normal work week. So Saturday mornings it would have to be for this particular desire. We kept forgetting, or the weather would not cooperate, or some other plan would abort the opportunity, until this Saturday, when after already sitting inside reading for a half hour it dawned on me that we could be doing the same outside. So we did.

Our backyard is nice. We live in an apartment, so it's shared, but our fourplex is wide and long, which means the backyard is the same. It is grass and trees, shrubs, raised garden boxes, an abandoned chicken coop and some garden beds inside the old run. Flowers and vegetables and some raspberries and blackberries and blueberries. Rose bushes. It is not the exact yard we would have if we had planted it ourselves —it would have less or no grass instead, lots of natives and flowers and food—but it still is nice. And there's a brick patio at the back end, half beneath the yard's largest tree, one edge lined with potted plants Kate tends and nurtures, with the middle of the patio sporting an arrangement of plastic lawn chairs and a couple small tables. It was there we planted ourselves that morning.

Not only is the backyard nice, it holds a good amount of life once you grow still and look and listen for it. Much of it is insect life: bees and flies and yellow jackets, the occasional dragonfly and a wide variety of pollinators, little critters I can't always identify but that I always enjoy. Then there are the birds: songbirds, hummingbirds, crows, little finches or something like finches flicking into one of the drying sunflower stalks and prying seeds from its head. (I need to get better at my bird identification, but mostly I just enjoy watching them. I like to know their names, but it's not critical.) And of course, the squirrels. While we sit out there, one of them goes running along the top board of our back fence, a large walnut hanging from her mouth, just feet away from us and increasing her speed as she passes, tinged with frantic. Both of us watch it go and Kate comments on the critter.

Behind her—Kate, that is, not the squirrel—is half our garden, planted in the old chicken run. Tomato vines sprawl within the beds, a romanesco squash plant holds its (unfortunately downy mildew-covered) leaves out to the sunlight, and cucumbers crawl up a wire mesh fence. Many of their leaves have yellowed; I'm not sure if it's from lack of nutrients or something else and, if I'm being honest here, I haven't bothered to research. We still are receiving cucumbers off them, though probably not as many as we might hope. I suppose I should pay closer attention, but it has been a hurried, busy summer. Still, I'll remember this next year, their yellowing in the corner I chose for them. The first year, I attempted to grow them along the fence and that did not work. This year has been better, even if imperfect. Perhaps next year I'll find the true sweet spot, the patch of ground that will keep us in cucumbers all summer long.

Next to the cucumbers is our rhubarb, planted the year before. Half a bed away is a tangled mass of dying bush beans, their final shells left to yellow and the beans inside to dry; I may yet harvest them either for next year's seed or, more likely, to cook and eat in a future meal.

There are four tomato plants in this section. For some lucky critter, they have been offering up a nightly feast. It started out modest: a missing Sungold cherry tomato, only the second to ripen, and which I had been eyeing one day and found gone the next. Then, cruelly, a large red slicer. Again, it being early, I had my eye on it as it stood out as one brightening patch of red in a sea of green tomatoes, the first slicer to ripen. I proudly called Kate over to show her one day as I felt it about ready to harvest and, grabbing it to tilt forward for her to see, felt my fingers sink into an open tomato wound. The back side of the fruit was eaten away, juicy flesh exposed to the air. I was devastated.

Since then, it has not stopped. As the tomatoes ripen, some of them appear half-eaten shortly before I would harvest them. Every time I find a new one, it's a tiny devastation. And now it has started to spread, onward to the squash and even the rhubarb leaves. A knife in the heart. Elsewhere, meanwhile, some critter is apparently sated. A squirrel, I suspect, though I don't know for sure. But perhaps the same one who ran past us along the top of the fence, walnut in mouth. Maybe not, but I wonder.

I am reading *Braiding Sweetgrass* by Robin Wall Kimmerer. It is a beautiful book, a collection of musings and essays that twine around indigenous knowledge, ethnobotany, plant biology, and personal experience. I sit in my plastic chair, with a mug of coffee beside me, the book in my lap. Kate sits opposite me. The squirrel runs by. Birdsong ebbs and flows around us. The sun shines, then is muted by wispy clouds, waiting to burn off. A slight breeze trembles the leaves above us and chills our skin. The buzz of insects arises behind me, centered on the potted plants and their flowers. It is far richer than when we sat indoors on the couch, though that is a nice way to spend a quiet Saturday morning as well.

I read about honorable harvests and Kimmerer's thoughts and words and deeds echo within me. The ideals she writes about speak to me; some of them I feel I live up to and others I don't. It makes a difference to be reading the book outside, especially with the garden—with those preyed-upon tomatoes—in view. Thoughts of them have been tugging at me intermittently for weeks, my minimal efforts to dissuade the tomato thief having failed. Kate read online that the scent of blood meal may help; a fine garden amendment anyway, I purchased a box and put some out in small plastic dishes. No luck. Still tomatoes turned half-eaten overnight and eventually I will mix the blood meal into a slurry and add it to my basil in the hopes of giving it a late-season boost.

I have not gone deeper down the rabbit hole, so to speak. We are getting tomatoes out of the garden now that so many are ripening, but still we lose a good number and still it pains me. We don't eat tomatoes the rest of the year and the ones from the garden, picked at the height of ripeness, are the best. I don't want to lose them.

Yet there's always a tax. The land deserves a portion as well, and I assume it will take it one way or another. But that knowledge is only a certain amount of cold comfort, and as I see more and more tomatoes half eaten—or, more dispiriting, see three or four with small nibbles taken out of them, as though the thief must spread around his assault—I feel an occasional flicker of a desire to kill this beast. It is an overwrought response, of course. We hardly are going to starve if some of our tomatoes go missing. Yet the desire flares, and I tamp it down by thinking about how I would quench such a blood thirst. I refuse to use poison. I do not want to use a trap. Honestly, I do not want to kill whatever creature is eating on the garden. I just want my tomatoes.

But are they mine? And if so, how many? To what percentage do I get to lay claim? To what amount of the land's productivity am I entitled? I see no clear answer to these questions, and my comfort, my lack of real *need* for the food in my garden, does my case no favors. *There's always a tax*, I remind myself again. I just wish I better understood the tax collector. Maybe we could work out a deal.

As I read in *Braiding Sweetgrass* about the indigenous approach to harvesting sweet-grass—which is to take half of the blades, never more—and its positive impact on the health of the sweetgrass population, a thought occurs to me. I don't understand the tomato thief's behavior. Perhaps this is not surprising, given that I am human and the perpetrator is not. Still, it confounds me. The most maddening part is how he chews on so many of the tomatoes. He does not eat an entire one and leave sated, but instead chews a bit on one, then a bit on another one, then on to a third. It provides no more food for him, but ensures plenty of loss for me. Perhaps if he simply ate one tomato and left me two or three that have ripened, I would not be so frustrated; but no, he must spread around the misery, taking, to my mind, so very much. An unfair tax, if one will.

Perhaps not, though. I suddenly wonder if this is a strike toward something deeper and more important than my own frustration, some kind of beneficial strategy. Perhaps by eating a bit of multiple tomatoes rather than all of one, the squirrel is ensuring future tomatoes. These half eaten tomatoes, still half full of seeds, will rot and fall from the vine, spilling their seeds to the ground below. New tomatoes will seed themselves and the next year another harvest will arise.

Is this possible? Perhaps. More likely, my mind casts around for ways to make sense of a world that, in this particular instance, confounds me. Still, it gives me pause and stirs a different kind of respect for the tomato thief, or at least a grudging acknowledgment that his actions are not likely designed to infuriate me—that, indeed, he almost surely does not think of me at all. He is simply eating, in his own particular way. And so, mulling this reality, I decide to accept it: I will not fight this squirrel. I will pick the tomatoes a little earlier, a little underripe, to retrieve more before they are eaten, and I will otherwise accept the loss. It is the way of the world, after all, and each gardening season presents its own unique challenges. One can never forget that.

It feels good, this acquiescence. It is easy to mistake it as a defeat, especially in our industrial culture in which we demand that other living things act not as beings with their own thoughts and desires, but as machines placed upon the earth to serve us. But it is not a defeat; it is a willingness to live and let live within a context not so dire as to demand otherwise.

I sit with the decision, still in the backyard and with the book now set down beside me. Kate has gone back into the apartment to make breakfast and I am giving myself over to the yard around me, to whatever arises—which, as it happens, is a yellow jacket. It emerges from the ether (or perhaps the neighbor's yard) to begin to buzz around me, swooping in and out, seemingly interested but not particularly aggressive.

Still, I can't help but try to wave it away. My halfhearted motion does not do much but alter its flight path, and I resist the urge to whack more aggressively at the insect. Instead, still basking in the glow of my intended co-existence with the tomato thief, I simply stand from my chair and back a few feet away and watch. The yellow jacket does not come with me but instead continues to circle in place until, after a few moments, it settles upon my coffee mug, still perched on the small table next to my abandoned chair.

I wonder, on that warm and dry morning, if it simply wants a drink. Condensation beads on the mug. The yellow jacket crawls over it. I can't quite tell if it actually sips from the water, but again I form my theory. Truth, or just an attempt to make sense of the world? I don't know that it matters.

I watch the yellow jacket. From my position, free of its circling buzz or swooping dive bombs, my slight annoyance turns to an interest in the creature's actions. It crawls over the cup, takes flight, hovers, returns to the cup, crawls along its surface once more, and again launches itself into the air. I feel a small affection for the yellow jacket, and then it disappears. In allowing the insect a small bit of space and time, all has resolved itself.

From there, I take notice of my laundry line. When we first moved into the apartment, I would put it up and take it down with loads of laundry, but after awhile I just left them up throughout the year. I have two of them, one tied off between two trees and one tied off between one of those same trees and a bit of wire mesh fencing running off the old chicken coop, the same one the cucumbers climb. The lines have been up at least a year since I last took them down or moved them.

I know what that means. The tree has been growing, its branches extending themselves in diameter, but the laundry line . . . well, it's tied tight, and made of plastic. I suspect at this point it is biting into the tree, and as I begin to untie the first knots, I feel a pang of guilt. I have been meaning to do this for awhile and keep forgetting.

I struggle for a minute before loosening the line, but then it comes off to reveal an indentation in the tree branch, a ring of what looks like compressed bark. It is perhaps a millimeter deep. A small strangling, a failure on my part. I move to the other tree, the one with two lines tied off on different branches. I work on those for awhile, the plastic binds not wanting to come loose, but I eventually free the tree from their restrictions. Two more rings, two more abuses. I retie the lines in different places and leave them a bit more loose, though I need to tighten them somewhat to keep the lines from drooping too much. I touch each tree and apologize. I will have to move them sooner next time, and I hope that the tree is not too harmed by the plastic ties.

Perhaps I should put them up and take them down with our loads of laundry, but I use them so often. Or perhaps the tree would appreciate a natural fiber line instead.

Perhaps I should ask.

It is amazing how much I see and hear when I let myself watch and listen. Even in a city backyard, there is so much life. Basic observation shows how much the bees enjoy the flowering basil, borage and still-fresh sunflowers. The birds, meanwhile, prefer the drying sunflower heads beside it, flitting in and out from a nearby tree to snack on the formed seeds. The neighbor's cat—who has become quite the regular visitor via a hole in the corner of the chain link fence dividing our backyards —watches with interest. I have yet to see him pursue one of the birds, though, instead focusing his hunting on the grasshoppers in the yard, which seem abundant this year.

From a massive walnut tree in a yard not far beyond comes the sound of a squirrel gnawing on the tree's early harvest. Not long after, a trail of branches shake as the squirrel scrambles through them. On occasion, a murder of crows will settle into the same walnut tree as the evening draws toward darkness, and many summer mornings we wake up to their excitable chatter coming through our open bedroom windows. In the garden in the chicken coop, several small holes in the soil let loose a boil of tiny ants. A flush of weeds push their way from the ground. Volunteer tomato plants strive toward the sun while a stray fennel flowers. The other day, as I was hanging laundry, a *rat-a-tat-tat* caused me to look skyward; crouched in the crook of a branch, a Northern Flicker pecked away at the wood, searching out morsels. It paid little attention to me, despite my proximity, and I took a small break from laundry to watch and marvel.

There are aphids, ladybugs, bumblebees. Mud wasps and honeybees and mason bees. When you're still, you start to see them. Sometimes you don't even have to be still—they just take you by surprise and bring the stillness to you.

Not long ago, on a hot and dry day, I went out to water the garden. My irrigation system is not fancy, just a hose and a cheap plastic spray nozzle from the neighborhood hardware store. I started with my usual bed, soaking the kale and chard and parsley and basil, then moving on to the second garden box, sending down a cascade of water on the summer squash. Within a few seconds, a hummingbird appeared, zoomed up near to me and hovered in the air. He darted back and forth, surprisingly close, while I watched him in surprise. He landed on the top rung of a metal tomato cage next to the summer squash and I grew still, the squash now getting a good long drink but me not wanting to scare off my visitor. (Besides, what squash has ever complained of too much water?) Launching himself off the tomato cage, he darted in yet closer and, as I watched in mild amazement, dipped his long beak into the stream of water, not more than eighteen inches from my body and closer still to the hand holding the base of the spray nozzle.

Delighted by this visitation and hoping to prolong it rather than bring it to an abrupt end, I continued to hold the spray of water as still as I could. The hummingbird darted in several times for a drink, then flitted over and actually landed on the spray nozzle itself, inches from my hand. He rested only a moment before rising again into the air and then, as I grinned in a wild enjoyment at the display, he carefully dipped the bottom of his body into the flow of water, wetting and cooling his chest and belly, seemingly no more concerned about me than the garden plants below.

He zoomed off a moment later, presumably refreshed and reinvigorated. I finally moved the water off the squash and continued watering the garden, moving to the tomatoes. My mind buzzed with the display, though, and I gave a silent thanks for having experienced it.

I may have laughed aloud. What a delightful world.

That morning now has passed. The squirrel continues to at times pilfer our tomatoes —not to mention take bites of other random crops—but his interest seems to have waned. He eats fewer of them now and I imagine his hunger has moved on, at least partly, perhaps taking greater interest in the maturing walnuts. Tomatoes crowd our kitchen counter instead. This weekend may be the time for our annual feast: a cutting board spread with slices of tomatoes, with mozzarella and basil, salt and a bottle of olive oil at the ready and a slab of good bread from the nearby bakery at hand. We are ready. The bounty comes eventually, even when you have to share it.

Outside, the garden is still abuzz with insects. If anything, they seem even more abundant than before. Maybe they are entering into a frenzy of activity as the summer starts to draw to its close. Surely they can feel fall approaching. The other day I harvested our flowering basil so I could make pesto before leaving town. It was a fury of honey bees, their enthusiasm contagious. I felt bad as I snipped each flower, slowly reducing their banquet down from a feast to a scatter of leftovers. Luckily, there are other flowers nearby. It may be that they grumbled at my perceived greed, as I did with the squirrel; hopefully though, here at the end of the season, there is enough to go around and they found plenty of pollen elsewhere, just as our kitchen counter has turned into a sprawl of tomatoes. I want pesto in my freezer for winter, but I also want honey in the beehive, wherever it is, for winter. We all must eat, after all, and I want the bees to return next summer. Their presence is a pleasure I have no interest in losing.

It is surprising how a simple morning outside, or a brief break to water the garden, can make all this apparent. Simple thought and observation—a consideration of the non-human world, which equates to most of the world—can bring so much to the forefront of my mind. Sitting still, outside, with a cup of coffee in hand and a good book to stimulate my thoughts, brings the world into a sharper focus. And from a squirrel to a yellow jacket to a garden to a tree, from the birds to the bees to a hummingbird's mid-air bathing, from half-chewed tomatoes on the vine to whole ones on the kitchen counter—it all is a reminder of the abundance of this world. Not just an abundance for me, for my wife, for us, but for all the non-human creatures sharing our backyard with us, gnawing in the trees above, or waiting for a cascade of water to quench their thirst and cool their bodies. It makes me happy to be a part of it, to be a piece of that wild whole. And as the inevitable cold and rain and gray of fall sets in over the coming weeks, and more and more of my time is spent inside, I will aim to hold onto that sense of abundance, of diversity, of human and non-human and just how alive it all is when I only take a moment to stop and see, to grow still and listen and discover. To take my coffee outside, sit in the backyard, and see who arrives to say hello and remind me just how big this world is.

— Portland, Oregon
September 7, 2019

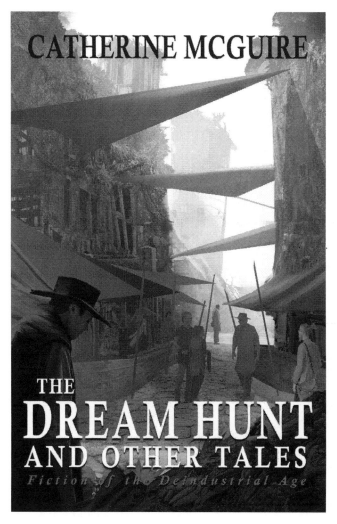

Into the Ruins is published quarterly by Figuration Press. We publish deindustrial science fiction that explores a future defined by natural limits, energy and resource depletion, industrial decline, climate change, and other consequences stemming from the reckless and shortsighted exploitation of our planet, as well as the ways that humans will adapt, survive, live, die, and thrive within this future.

One year, four issue subscriptions to *Into the Ruins* are $39. You can subscribe by visiting intotheruins.com/subscribe or by mailing a check made out to Figuration Press to:

Figuration Press / 3515 SE Clinton Street / Portland, OR 97202

To submit your work for publication, please visit intotheruins.com/submissions or email submissions@intotheruins.com.

All issues of *Into the Ruins* are printed on paper, first and foremost. Electronic versions will be made available as high quality PDF downloads. Please visit our website for more information. The opinions expressed by the authors do not necessarily reflect the opinions of Figuration Press or *Into the Ruins*. Except those expressed by Joel Caris, since this is a sole proprietorship. That said, all opinions are subject to (and commonly do) change, for despite the Editor's occasional actions suggesting the contrary, it turns out he does not know everything and the world often still surprises him.

EDITOR-IN-CHIEF
JOEL CARIS

DESIGNER
JOEL CARIS

WITH THANKS TO
JOHN MICHAEL GREER
OUR SUBSCRIBERS

SPECIAL THANKS TO
KATE O'NEILL

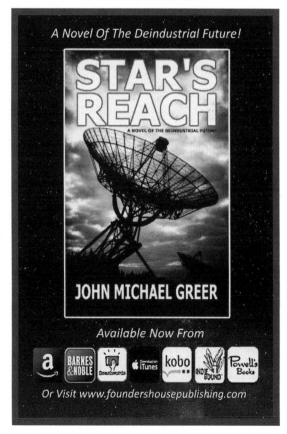

Contributors

JOEL CARIS is a gardener and homesteader, occasional farmer, passionate advocate for local and community food systems, sporadic writer, voracious reader, sometimes prone to distraction and too attendant to detail, a little bit crazy, a cynical optimist, and both deeply empathetic toward and frustrated with humanity. He is your friendly local editor and publisher. As a reader of this journal and perhaps other writings of his, he hopes you don't too easily tire of his voice and perspective. He lives in Oregon with his amazing wife, who consistently delights him.

ALISTAIR HERBERT writes from a little house on the edge of Todmorden in West Yorkshire, where he lives with his partner and two young children. He studied creative writing at the University of Manchester and now works part time for a local government organisation —an occupation which has largely kept him out of trouble for thirteen years. His work has previously appeared in Comma Press' *Parenthesis* anthology, as well as the Summer 2017, Winter 2018, Spring 2018, and Summer 2018 issues of *Into the Ruins*.

Working in multiple genres, **LAWRENCE BUENTELLO** has published over 100 short stories and innumerable poems in journals, magazines, and anthologies, many of which can be found in several volumes of collected fiction and poetry. He is also the author or co-author of several novels. Buentello lives in his hometown of San Antonio, Texas.

DAVID ENGLAND is a ponderer, generalist, and student-of-everything who makes his home in a pleasant working-class community along the western shore of Lake Michigan, where he lives with his wife Anne, her amazing artwork, and the cacophony of voices in his head telling him what to write next. His stories have appeared in the anthology *Vintage Worlds*, the online 'zine *Tales to Astound*, as well as the quarterlies *MYTHIC* and *Into the Ruins*.

CLINT SPIVEY teaches English as a foreign language. During his free time he works on a small rice farm. His fiction has appeared in *Into the Ruins*, *Aurora Wolf*, and the anthology *Vintage Worlds: Tales of the Old Solar System*.

W. JACK SAVAGE is a retired broadcaster and educator. He is the author of seven books, including *Imagination: The Art of W. Jack Savage*. To date, more than fifty of Jack's short stories and over seven hundred of his paintings and drawings have been published worldwide. Jack and his wife Kathy live in Monrovia, California. Jack is, as usual, responsible for this issue's cover art. He can be found at wjacksavage.com.

VIOLET BERTELSEN is an herbalist, farmhand and amateur historian currently living in the northeastern United States. While a child, the woods befriended and educated Violet, who proved to be an eager student. She spent her young adulthood in a haze, wandering the vast expanses of North America trying to find the lost fragments of her soul in deserts, hot springs and railyards. Now older and more sedate, she likes to spend her time talking with trees, reading history books, laughing uproariously with fellow farmhands, drinking black birch tea and, on occasion, writing science fiction stories. Violet's work has also appeared in the Winter 2018, Spring 2019, and Summer 2019 issues of *Into the Ruins* and in the old solar system anthology *Vintage Worlds* (Founders House Publishing).

MATTHEW SPAUR is a marketing consultant, former newspaper publisher, and a double threat MFA + MBA. Recently, he designed and wrote the spellbinding B2B marketing whitepaper *Making The Most of Manager Time*. He has also published works in *South Dakota Review*, *Owen Wister Review*, *Wisconsin Review*, *Willow Springs*, and a magazine called *Heliotrope* but probably not the one you might have seen. Lots of people name their magazine *Heliotrope*. If he had to do it all over again, he'd probably be a graphic designer and photographer. Or an economist. Maybe both.

J.D. MOYER lives in Oakland, California, with his wife, daughter, and mystery-breed dog. He writes science fiction, produces electronic music in two groups (Jondi & Spesh and Momu), runs a record label (Looq Records), and blogs at jdmoyer.com. His short stories have appeared in *The Magazine of Fantasy & Science Fiction*, *Strange Horizons*, *The InterGalactic Medicine Show*, *Cosmic Roots And Eldritch Shores*, and *Compelling Science Fiction*. His novelette *The Icelandic Cure* won the 2016 Omnidawn Fabulist Fiction contest. His Reclaimed Earth science fiction series is published by Flame Tree Press.

LETTERS TO THE EDITOR

Dear Editor,

Karl North's article on what he calls the Gothic Age has one major flaw: he has taken a thousand years of Medieval history, a history which covered all of Western and Central Europe, thrown in the Burning Times, which took place when the Medieval order was crumbling and badly broken along religions lines, and conflated them into one big dark and evil Gothic Age. It's as if the Scholars in the days of Star's Reach were to roll all of United States history, from the landing at Jamestown to the Fall of the Empire, and equated the entire shebang with the darkest moments of the slavery days.

This is not an unusual practice among those those who have not studied the period in great detail, but let's look at the incidents under a magnifying glass. Early period law codes in England, for example, copying what they had of Roman law, forbade all sorts of divination and magic, but in practice, very few people were convicted of maleficia, and an early Pope decreed that "some deluded women" believed they rode at night with Diana and practiced witchcraft, but that was silly superstition and not to be taken seriously by good Christians. The King of Norway converted his nation to Christianity by fire and sword; both Ireland and Iceland converted peacefully—Iceland, in fact, by popular vote.

It was a time of crusades against the Infidel (1095-1492, the latter exclusive to Spain and part of the extended Reconquista) and the extermination of presumed heretics (1209-1229). After the Cathars were put down with fire and sword in the 13th Century, the Inquisition was established to root out heretics, with the Dominicans ("The Hounds of God"—a Latin pun, 'domini canus') their shock troops. But anyone who thinks Everyman and his family were living in a totalitarian nightmare of Gothic gloom should dip into Canterbury Tales—an authentic period source!

Fast-forward to the notorious Burning Times (1486-1650), which does reflect North's thesis quite well. As he said, troubled times in every respect. According to historian Ronald Hutton, "The scholarly consensus on the total number of executions for witchcraft ranges from 40,000–60,000."

Your fear of conservative or fundamentalist Christianity today in the United States is shared by many, and the statements and in many cases deeds of some it its practitioners gives us good cause to fear. I would like to note, however, the cyclical nature of this sort of religious/political fundamentalism.

Some historians claim to see a thirty year swing from liberal to conservative, from emphasis on politics, to emphasis on saving your individual soul. I can only say that the Gothic streak in American history comes into full bloom during a Crisis era, such as the 1930s, and again today. (2001-2024?)

As a side note, Robert Heinlein's collection *Revolt in 2100*, part of his *Future History* series, predicted a loud-mouth televangelist elected President in 2012 and the theocratic regime (admirably described forty years later by Margaret Atwood in *The Handmaid's Tale*) overthrown one long lifetime later. No longer, in fact, than the Soviet Union lasted in our own timeline. Heinlein knew a lot about Gothic America. He also understood the cycles of history extremely well, for all that he was also the primary author of of the Great Faustian Monofuture.

Patricia Mathews
Gainesville, Florida

Dear Editor,

I just want to say that I, like you, see collapse as a long process, not a sudden fall off a cliff. My heart breaks when I see what Dorian, truly a Category 6 monster, did to the Bahamas. Those islands will never recover to what they were before this tragedy. We see in the island of Great Abaco what happens when an infrastructure of power, food and water, built over decades, is taken away in a matter of

hours; we may have the resources and ability to recover from this event, and the next one, but we won't be able to recover forever. In similar fashion, we see other pockets of collapse already appearing: sunny day floods in Miami, the toxic water issues in so many United States cities like Flint and Newark, the recurrent flooding along the Mississippi and Missouri rivers, and hopefully we won't soon be talking about Los Angeles, San Francisco or Seattle and the unlikely possibility that they will fully recover from the "Big One."

We are so reliant upon getting our sustenance from technology we can't easily imagine what it would be like to lose it. This imagining is what makes *Into the Ruins* such a great service, such a great read. I look forward to many more years of issues, and thank you, and our authors, so very much.

Derek Tennant
San Jose, California

Dear Editor,

It's always a delight to read a story by G. Kay Bishop. To me, "Freedom" in the summer issue [*Into the Ruins: Summer 2019* (Issue #13)] is especially enjoyable and admirable. Every word in the story carries full weight, and conversations quickly get to the point of the matter without seeming abrupt. When Bishop describes person, place or thing it is always the essence that is illuminated.

"Freedom," a coming-of-age story, is sited in an undefined time and placed in a world of scarcity. Bishop captures the angst of unrealizable adolescent dreams and the un-relievable ache of a mother unable to help her son. Time and place are irrelevant; the feelings are universal.

Bishop isn't a softy, but also isn't judgmental. The story's end isn't kind, nor is it unnecessarily mean; it just is. It's the way things turned out.

You know. That's life.

Al Sevcik
Tampa, Florida

Dear Editor,

Touching on the role of magic in the deindustrial age—and certainly on spirituality—I'd like to relate a recent experience of mine.

The other day, I took a few minutes during my lunch at work, as I often do, to sit in meditation. The utility where I work has its facilities on the shore of Lake Michigan, so I need only walk a short ways to reach the beach. I frequently sit on a small rise overlooking the shore, with a variety of shoreline vegetation and associated insect life between me and the water. I had seated myself, gone through my brief breathing exercises, and settled into the moment, allowing my gaze to rest softly on the scene in front of me.

On more than one occasion, I've been given insights by my patron goddess, most definitely an earth deity but who has declined to tell me her name. I refer to her alternately as Gaia, Ge, or Whomever She May Be. In any event, She is who She is.

As I sat, I saw a shadow dart across the sand and I looked up, searching the sky for the bird which had cast that shadow. There was none. The sky was blue and clear, with no birds in sight whatsoever. It took me a moment, but I realized that what I had seen had not been a bird's shadow on the sand in the middle distance, but rather a dragonfly in the nearer distance, flying at just the right level and just the right distance away so as to appear to have been a shadow cast on the sand much further behind it.

Now, one of the traditional meanings of the dragonfly is illusion and deception. As I reflected on this experience, that quiet voice in my head —often the mechanism by which She speaks to me—said, "The thing you look for does not exist."

And it all clicked. In my pondering of our deindustrial future, I have always sought to find a way, some way, to mitigate the worst of what is to come. A pro-active, methodical set of policies by which our nation could extract itself from its empire and buffer the political and economic stresses that lay ahead as this century unfolds. A managed way down.

It doesn't exist. That is, I'm asking that people, humans, be something other than what we are: clever toolmakers, but inevitably short-sighted creatures who respond to the immediate. Our "way down" will be what it was always going to be, and what it was always going to be is a sequence of haphazard, ad hoc, band-aid solutions strung together, each designed to address some immediate crisis, but with no overarching plan, no coherent strategy, no managed way down.

And moreover, tying back to the other theme to which I've been directed, by expending my energy searching for this thing that doesn't exist, I am forgoing spending that energy on my own life, on my own personal journey, my own path, which is far more relevant than I tend to give it credit for. (One of the things She had told me, years ago, was: "You focus on that which is unimportant and that which is truly important you miss completely.")

So, once again, it is the here and the now that matters. Our own personal journeys into the beginnings of this deindustrial age.

David England
Two Rivers, Wisconsin

Dear Editor,

I rarely read contemporary novels (despite attempting to write novels myself, I suspect and perhaps even hope that the form is on its way out, having enjoyed a comfortable couple of centuries already as the dominant medium of expression), but I picked up Richard Powers' *The Overstory* from my char-ity shop's bookshelf last week and ploughed through it in about three days. It might not be perfect—the second half is a little too tidy for me in places—but the novel as a whole more than compensates; beautiful, compassionate writing about people, which somehow turns the trick of repeatedly altering perspective to make those people into a kind of background for the arcs of world history which might be understood by some of our planet's other species. It's a novel about trees and activists, but also about one of the crucial questions humans are beginning to wrestle with again after a long holiday: how do we as a species listen to the rest of the world and find our right place in it?

One of the ideas the novel digs into quite deeply is that of herd mentality; it asks how it is that some people succeed in seeing through the damaging cultural stories of a time, while most do not. In our context, if so many people are comprehensively blinded by social instinct to the ways that their own lives cause ecological catastrophe, and similarly unable to make reasonable judgements about planning for the futures they're actually likely to see, why can a few people see it at all? If it's so ingrained to allow social influences to override individual doubts, how does anyone have the radical idea at all, let alone find other people to share it? What makes those few people different? What allows the very first visionaries to see at all, and what enables the first few followers who come around to their way of seeing to come around, when everyone else can't?

The novel offers answers in the forms of its characters. I wonder what other people think about these questions. For me, I think I've long been a bit of an outsider, and long felt ambivalent about being invited in to the bigger party. I remember reading the Dark Mountain manifesto in 2009 and feeling like a lot of things I didn't understand all came into focus—but then I remember the same feeling in 2006 when I re-read my first "practice" novel, which, nominally about a teenager trying to find a future in a fading city, and a divorcee trying to bury her own questions in a home improvement project, turned out to be all about they ways people blind themselves to truths which ought to be obvious. Even then I knew our central cultural stories were flawed; I just failed to arrive at a conscious diagnosis.

Then I remember the music I was listening to as a teenager at the turn of the century: bands like Godspeed You! Black Emperor, who played apocalyptic post-rock around poems of system collapse ("The car is on fire and there's no driver at the wheel . . . we are trapped in the belly of this machine and the machine is bleeding to death . . ."), and Radiohead, whose three records between 1997 and 2001 extended and inverted the tech-fetishism of the time into a kind of anti-human emptiness. I begin to think that filtering these messages through the natural adolescent unease

I went through around that time was really how I first began to learn to see the world behind our culture's stories about it. I wonder now if the adolescent unease was a crucial ingredient for me, without which I wouldn't have seen anything—my substitute for the near-death experience of one character in *The Overstory*, or the crippling loss experienced by another—or if it was incidental.

I wonder what other people think about this—how do people arrive at stories outside the cultural norm? is it a fool's errand to look for common threads in those stories?—and, naturally, it's hard to find people to ask, given that I'm asking about something a lot of people don't even see.

Best wishes,

Alistair Herbert
Todmorden, United Kingdom

Into the Ruins welcomes letters from our readers. We encourage thoughtful commentary on the contents of this issue, the themes of the magazine, humanity's future, and other relevant subjects. Readers may email their letters to editor@intotheruins.com or mail them to:

Joel Caris
Figuration Press
3515 SE Clinton Street
Portland, OR 97202

10 Billion

A Graphic Novel Based on the Story by John Michael Greer

Available November 2019

For more information visit next10billion.com

STORIES

The Sacramento Sea
by J.D. Moyer

MY HUSBAND LIONEL WAS DONE. Ninety-five was young for a man to die, but I figured he'd checked every item on his list. He was camped out on the living room couch, looking a shade yellow but otherwise in good spirits.

"I can charge up the motorboat, take you to Sacramento to get a new liver," I offered.

"Would have been a good idea two months ago, Hannah. No time to grow it now."

"Sure—that's why I suggested it back then." I shook my head. Stubborn old fart.

"How much longer you gonna stick around, young lady?" he asked. Our little joke, me being twenty years his junior.

"What do you mean? Here in town? Or how much longer am I going to live?" He shrugged. "Either. Both."

"I'm not moving to the city, if that's what you're asking. Somebody's gotta take care of Rachel and Tiger. And keep an eye on Sam." Rachel and Tiger are the goat and cat, respectively. Sam runs the survivalist compound down Pike Road, king of his own domain. Though as far as I know he's the only one left. The last of his followers skedaddled when Highway 84 went under.

"Don't live too long. You'll get lonely." Lionel squeezed my hand, grinned.

"I'll live as long as I damn well please." I punched his shoulder. Then, earnestly (we switched modes quickly—always could), "I don't have any big plans, but I'm not done yet. Maybe life still has a few adventures in store."

"If not, you'll make some."

Two days later he was dead. I buried him on the little hill out back like we'd planned, in the coffin he'd built himself. Used some driftwood that was kicking around the yard to make a cross, carved his name: *Lionel Hemsly, 1978-2073*.

‡‡

The Sacramento-San Joaquin River Delta flooded gradually. Most of the levees that broke (in cyclone Gil in '44, or the wet winter of '62) were privately maintained, and what cash-strapped sugar beet or alfalfa farmer could afford to get them fixed? As for the state of California, they ponied up to save Isleton due to its vaunted historical landmark status, but left the rest of us little towns to fend. Which meant converting cropland into fish farms (best case scenario) or just getting the hell out and starting over in some podunk town in the Sierra foothills (or Denver, or some other mile-high city, for those that could afford it).

Lionel and I held on. No kids, parents long dead, him an only child, me estranged from my sister. Courtland was our life. We considered ourselves stewards, the old guard, making sure everyone got out safe. Took care of the animals, as long as they lived, or until they went feral and didn't need us.

That reminds me—gotta do something about that pack of wild dogs. They almost got to Rachel the other day.

What the hell will I eat? Lionel used to take the boat over down to Isleton for supplies, or sometimes east to Laguna for big-ticket items. But I'm of a mind to fend for myself. How much do one old lady and a cat need? Tiger supplements his kibble with mice and bugs (but no songbirds—they see him coming from a mile away with his rainbow collar).

Plenty of pears and apples most of the year—and cherries in May—from the old orchards that belonged to Lionel's cousins before they took off. Technically, I may *own* those orchards now, though I don't think anybody is keeping track. So I'm good on fruit. And I've got tomatoes, chard, onions, garlic, sweet peppers, and beets from the backyard. Tomorrow I'll raid Mrs. Thornton's greenhouse, see what's there.

As for milk and cheese, I'll go without. Rachel's the only goat on the island so there's no chance of her getting pregnant and producing milk. Those who had dairy cows took them with, and even if there *was* a herd of wild bovines, I wouldn't mess with them.

So for protein, it'll be mostly eggs. I've been caring for Mrs. Thornton's hens and they've been providing. No reason I can't keep that going.

And fish, hopefully. I can ration the canned sardines and salmon to last at least a couple months. By then I should be an old hand at catching my own. I've heard about monster sturgeon in Prospect Slough. It's all one big slough now, from 113 to Highway 5, so those prehistoric protein packs should be swimming right near my waterfront property.

I won't starve. If I get desperate, I'll hit up Sam. He's got years of dried provisions in his bunker, and he's the only one there to eat it.

Dealt with the wild dogs today. Stood in the front yard leaning over the wooden fence with a handful of cat kibble—wanted to see if any of them would eat out of my hand (had a machete in the other, just in case). A dirty yellow-and-white mutt —maybe a collie/lab mix—came right up, licked my palm clean. The other seven or eight hung back snarling.

I opened the gate and let her in. Decided to call her Lion, after Lionel. The rest I treated to a big bowl of peanut butter mixed with rat pellets. Sorry it had to be that way, but this island is too small for a pack that big.

Haven't found the bodies yet, but that bowl was empty this morning. Lion seems none the wiser, spent the night on Lionel's couch as if she owned it. The cat camped out on top of the china cupboard and glared at me.

Couple weeks later I took a walk to Sam's place, carrying my bucket, with Lion in tow. Sam greeted me from behind the scope of his Browning from fifty meters, as always. I waved from the top of his long driveway with my free hand, waited for him to come meet me, as is his preferred protocol.

"Did I miss any rioters or looters?" I asked cheerfully. Sam is an A-1 ass but I was lonely enough to feel happy at the sight of him.

"Nope. Not yet. Who's this?" He eyed the dog warily. Lion wagged his tail. "Stupid idea—an extra mouth to feed, in times like these," he said, scratching Lion's head.

"Yep."

"So what brings you here? Run out of food already?"

"Nope. Plenty to eat." I took the lid off my bucket, pulled out my catch. "Learning to fish, too. Caught myself . . . well . . . this." I held up the big striped bass. "Should we fry it up?"

Sam's face lit up. He slung his rifle over his shoulder and launched into a fishing lecture. Forty minutes later we were drinking bourbon and eating fried bass.

"How do you think they're doing in the big cities?" My reception had dropped to zero right around when Lionel died. We were totally cut off, news-wise.

Sam scowled. "Pretty grim by now, I imagine. Flooding, sewers overflowing, poison water, food shortages. Disease, death, and mayhem."

"Sacramento was fine last I heard. The water's only up a meter or two."

Sam patted the Browning, always at arm's reach. "We're safer here. You're a fool if you head to the city."

I shrugged. I didn't necessarily agree, but I had no desire to visit Sac or Stockton or Oakland, or across the bay to San Francisco. Sam was poor company, but he wasn't *no* company, and I didn't need much. I rubbed my bare foot on Lion's belly, under the table.

Sam sent me home with a twenty-pound bag of rice and a milk carton full of cooking oil. "You and the pooch should try to fatten up a little. You both got too many ribs showin'."

Sam hasn't seen my ribs or any other part of my body, but I took his point. I'd been shocked at the sight of own reflection lately, a tan old lady with sharp cheekbones.

Snagged my first sturgeon, only to have it stolen. Took the motorboat out to what used to be Prospect Slough—I guess now one might call it the western side of the Sacramento Sea. Armed with book knowledge and fishing gear I'd scavenged from Mrs. Thornton's garage (once belonging to the long-deceased Mr. Thornton), it took me less than an hour to hook the finned beast. I was reeling it in, inch-by-inch, could just see it thrashing below the surface, when a big gray thing swam up and ripped it right off my line.

For the next ten minutes I watched a pair of dolphins frolicking, eating my lunch. If their digits weren't fused into fins they would have been giving me the finger. I laughed it off—dolphins are a delight even when they've just robbed you blind. Didn't know they had a taste for freshwater fish. I scooped up some water and tasted it, something I hadn't done for years. Saltier than I remembered. Not seawater salty, but brackish.

Checked the county map when I got home and it all made sense. I'd been fishing right over what used to be the Sacramento River Deep Water Ship channel, running from Sac to the bay. The water isn't more than a few feet deep in the rest of this new sea, but that channel gave those dolphins all the room they need for their inland tour.

I wonder what else might swim to Courtland.

Got my answer to that question sooner than expected. U.S. Coast Guard paid me a visit this morning. I heard them from a mile off, watched them dock at the bridge that connects to what's left of Paintersville. I was worried Sam might take a potshot and get himself killed, but I guess he decided to hole up.

A handsome brown-skinned bearded fella and a mannish young woman walked around the island for half an hour yelling "Halloooo!" like fools before I showed my face and asked them how I could be of service. The gentleman introduced himself as Bradley Swift and tried to turn the tables on me, asked me how *he* could be of service, specifically in regards to evacuating my old butt from this island. *Condemned for human habitation* was the phrase he used, I believe. I guess some nosy concerned citizen spotted me on a fishing expedition and followed me with a mini-drone, ratted me out to the boat jockeys.

I told Bradley I was just fine where I was and unless he was prepared to drag me away by my gray ponytail, the status quo would prevail. Lion growled at him for emphasis. Bradley mumbled something about exemption paperwork and waiver of liability and I nodded as if I was listening.

"You from the Alameda base?" I asked as they were walking away.

"Golden Gate," said the woman.

"Is it rough, in the cities?" Left it vague—didn't want to let on that I hadn't read the news in eights months.

She looked confused. "What do you mean?"

"We're hanging in there," said Bradley. Did he give her a nudge?

"Well, thanks for checking up on me."

"Here, hold on to this," said the butch lady, handing me a walkie-talkie. "It's got a good range. If it runs out of batteries, just shake it."

"Thanks."

Didn't tell them about Sam. That's a can of bullets that doesn't need opening.

Months passed, days getting shorter and nights colder. The rains would be coming soon. I charged up my tablet and the motorboat engine battery pack (solar panels are still working, for now), packed up some dried pears and smoked fish, told Lion we were going on an adventure. Tiger glared at me from the fireplace mantel while we got ready. Still hasn't forgiven me for adopting the dog.

Took the boat northeast, toward Laguna, until my tablet flickered to life and synchronized with the mother ship. I'll admit my heart was racing as I checked the news. I knew I wasn't the last woman on Earth, but how bad was it?

Confusion: celebrity names I didn't recognize, companies I'd never heard of, even *countries* I'd never heard of. What was the African Equatorial Alliance? Was Iran called New Persia now? And who in the hell were Jadyn Firecat and Pedro Sandoz?

Lion snored in the bottom of the boat while I drilled into the details. After a couple hours I'd discovered our nation was still muddling along, with Sam's dire predictions of total collapse having not yet come to pass.

Hurricanes were still slamming the Eastern Seaboard and the southern states every few months. Most Floridians has just given up and moved.

Island communities had it the worst, and some had been abandoned entirely.

Refugee camps had turned into vast refugee tent cities.

California was going to have a wet, cold, windy winter, with a cyclone named Larry coming as far north as the San Francisco Bay.

That was enough news for the year. I was irritated with myself for getting sucked into Sam's apocalyptic predictions. Things were grim *here*, and a few other places, but not everywhere. I turned off the tablet, shared the rest of the smoked fish with Lion, and pointed the boat back home. Would Sam want to be brought up to date? Maybe he preferred imagining the world falling apart while he polished his Browning and ate canned Gro-Beef.

Two of Mrs. Thornton's chickens are dead. Necks broken, half-eaten. My first thought was wild dogs—maybe a few of them had survived—but the coop had been latched shut. Prints in the mud confirmed my next guess: raccoons.

Funny thing is, I haven't seen raccoons on the island, well, since we *became* an island. So unless they've been hiding, they swam here. That's a *long* swim, from any direction, but I remember something about raccoons swimming to Angel Island, in the bay, centuries ago.

I could try to trap them, poison them. But I feel bad about killing those dogs. We're all just animals here, trying to survive.

But from now on the chickens spend the night in the house. Tiger won't like it, but he'll have to deal. He can choose to be a feral cat anytime he pleases. Until then I'll just tolerate his resentful gaze.

I haven't been outside in two days. Rain, pounding on the roof, a continuous deluge. Lion huddles close to me, terrified. Rachel is cooped up in the garage, restlessly clattering her hooves. I have no idea where Tiger is. Hiding out somewhere dry, I hope.

Still raining. Windy too, though I'm sure the coast is getting the worst of it. I came downstairs this morning to a foot of water in the living room and kitchen. I checked on the goat in the garage. Rachel was fine, calmly perched on an empty wine barrel. Took some work to get her down into the water, then upstairs. Lion tried to help, barking and nipping. Now I've got a wet dog, a pissed-off goat, a missing cat, and no power. Not sure if the solar batteries are ruined or just dead. No power means no hot water, and no potable water either once the tank is empty (the well went bad years ago). So I'm rationing both food and drink. I'm cold too, wearing most of my clothes and a blanket for good measure.

Used my last clean towels to get Lion and Rachel half-dry. The animals are passive, pliant, trusting me to get us through this. I hope Tiger is okay.

Still raining. The water is a third of the way up the stairs. From the window I watched a wave sweep away Lionel's driftwood cross. When the rain stops the water will recede, but what will be left?

A dry, sunny day, finally. A relief to get out of my bedroom. "Barnyard" would be a euphemistic description of the smell at this point. I put on Lionel's old waders, mucked and squelched my way through the living room, dragging a reluctant Rachel behind me at the end of a rope. With some help from the dog, we got the goat outside and to the only dry ground: Lionel's burial hillock. The goat will have to mark his grave until I find something more permanent.

Got my hatchet, chopped down a young willow and stripped its branches. Needed a pole for the boat. The motorboat was still there, filled with water but not quite sunk. After an hour of bailing, I poled off with three goals in mind. One: find Tiger. Two: check on Sam. Three: tour what was left of the island and make my decision.

I passed the pear orchards on the way to Sam's place. I dragged the boat up a muddy slope, tied it off on the last standing fencepost. The trees were bare, the unpicked fruit having rotted off months ago. Still living, as far as I could tell, but would the brackish groundwater kill all the fruit trees? I wouldn't know until spring. I'd eaten enough pears to be sick of them by now, but what would I eat if they didn't come in?

Lion started barking, sprinted toward something flapping around in a big muddy puddle: a giant sturgeon, at least a six-footer, a prehistoric sea monster of a fish, covered in mud and flailing for its life. Without thinking I waded in and chopped at its head with my hatchet until it stopped moving.

I watched the seeping blood turn the water ruddy brown and wondered why I'd done it. To put the fish out of its misery? No, I was furious. The sturgeon was the rising Delta, taking back the land it had owned for millennia. Kicking me out of the only home I'd ever known. Out of guilt, I butchered the fish, put the dripping red steaks in plastic bags, hoped they'd still be good by the time I got home. Maybe Sam would want them.

We pushed off, poled around while I called "Tiger! Here kitty-kitty! Here Tiger!" Just as my voice was getting hoarse and my eyes tired from the bright winter light, we heard a pitiful mewling from high in a sprawling oak. Lion spotted him first but had the sense to stay quiet, just pointed her nose. I called and cajoled for half an hour but the damn cat just made mournful sounds and glared at me resentfully. I'm too old to climb trees—he'll have to come down when he's ready. I'm just relieved to know he's not drowned and eaten by Triassic carnivorous fish, or murdered by amphibious raccoons.

My shoulders were burning with lactic acid by the time I reached Pike Road and Sam's long driveway. He wasn't there to greet me from behind his rifle scope. *Security slipping, Sam*, I thought, cracking myself up. *What if I was a looter or rioter?* But then I caught sight of the bloody hatchet in my belt loop and it didn't seem as funny.

"Sam, you there?" I yelled, banging on the steel door of the main house. He'd set up a low wall of sandbags and it seemed to have worked for the most part—his weedy lawn was wet but my boots weren't sinking in. Still—I knew he kept most of his supplies on the basement level. Had it flooded? With him down there?

"Got some fresh sturgeon for you!"

I sat in his driveway and waited. I wasn't ready to break into his house and search for his body. Plus, he probably had the place booby-trapped. Lion whined anxiously, uncomfortable with me sitting still.

Sam appeared as a small figure at the top of his driveway, limping, carrying something in his hand. He was looking down and didn't notice me, even as he got close. I didn't get up or make noise—too tired—and Lion followed my cue.

He yelled when he finally saw me, lifted the black object in his hand.

"Easy there Sam! It's just me. I brought fish."

It wasn't a gun he was holding, but some electrical part. "Hey there Hannah. You scared the bejeezus out of me. I was over at Jensen's place. Borrowed his charge controller. Mine got fried in the rain—I got no power at all. Missed a nice sunny day, too." He squinted, looking west. The sunset almost made him look handsome, at least less old and less tired. Jensen had moved to Sacramento three years ago, had a fatal heart attack a year later. Had Sam forgotten?

I stood, feeling creaky, my joints audibly popping. Sam eyed my bloody hatchet. I'd tried to clean it on my shirt but only succeeded in smearing the blood around.

"It was a big one. A sturgeon. Stuck in a puddle, in the Hemsly orchard."

"*Your* orchard."

I shrugged. "Never took his name. And I never wanted to be a farmer."

He started to ask me a question, thought better of it, unlocked his door and invited me in. He built a fire in the courtyard pit from logs he'd kept dry, while listing off his supplies ruined by water: steel-cut oats, wheat flour, sugar. Dry-bin stuff in the basement, mostly. He berated himself for storing it down there—he'd been too confident in his own sealing abilities. The water always finds a way in. But the truth was he still had enough food to feed a dozen for years.

While Sam tended the fire I washed up in in his bathroom, cleaned the splattered sturgeon blood and mud off of my face and hands with cold water. I longed for a hot shower.

"I should have the power back up, by tomorrow," Sam said when I returned. He ran a sharp stick through the sturgeon steaks, positioned the spit carefully above the open flames. For a split second I considered inviting myself to move in. He had plenty of space, plenty of food. He wouldn't expect anything from me. Not even conversation.

But no. I was done living with other people.

"I might leave Courtland, Sam. The Coast Guard said they'd come get me if I wanted."

He watched the sturgeon steaks cook. "Where would you go?"

"Maybe Marin. Not as crowded there, I hear."

"Used to be rich folks in Marin. Might cost real money to live there."

"I'm a pear princess, remember?"

He frowned, quarter-turned the spit. The fish meat smelled good but I didn't have much appetite. Lion looked interested though, was acting friendly toward Sam.

"What you about you? Would you consider relocating? You know, things haven't gone totally to shit in the cities. Life goes on."

"Nah. I'll stay." I was surprised he didn't challenge me on the lack of apocalypse. Maybe he'd found a way to read the news himself.

"I'd leave you the walkie-talkie, case you got sick or something. Is your leg okay? Noticed you were favoring it."

He rubbed his hip. "Pulled something, yanking out Jensen's controller. But I've got the shortwave if I need it."

"Would you take care of the animals?"

He scratched Lion's head. "Sure, I'd take care of this one. I'm not really a cat person. I'd probably eat the goat."

You could trust the man to speak his mind.

I woke up the next morning (in my own bed, sheets still damp from wet dog) feeling resentful of Lionel. What had he meant, *Make some adventures*? I didn't want adventure. I wanted solar panels that worked, a warm dry house, my cat back.

"Tiger!" I called out the back door. "Here kitty!" I opened a can of sardines, emptied it into his bowl, left it on the back porch. If I saw a raccoon I'd stab it with a kitchen knife.

Mrs. Thornton's remaining chickens were dead, drowned in their own coop. I'd forgotten to bring the hens inside with all my worrying about the cat and the goat. I buried the chickens in muddy ground, worrying about water the whole time. The next big rain, and what I would drink.

Most of the sardines were eaten the next morning. I was cursing myself for wasting food on the stupid raccoons when I saw something bright across the yard. Tiger's songbird-protecting rainbow collar, snagged on a dried-up tomato vine.

So the cat had made his choice. Godspeed to the finches and wrens.

I shook the walkie-talkie until it lit up, scanned the channels. Mostly static. Finally some Coast Guard chatter. I held down the Transmit button, feeling awkward.

"Hello? Can anyone hear me? This is Hannah Birch. I spoke with a man by the name of Bradley Swift. Is he available?"

More chatter, codes I didn't understand. Then a clear, low female voice. "Hi, Hannah. This is Chief Petty Officer Jackson. I work with Ensign Swift—it was me who gave you the walkie-talkie. How can I help you?"

They pulled a tiny hovercraft practically right up to my house. I was all packed —just a couple bags of clothes and mementos, and the goat. I was hoping for Bradley but Hannah said he was working emergency relief in Hawaii—they'd been hit hard by Larry.

Rachel rode the hovercraft like a natural. That goat can roll with the punches. I looked back at Courtland Island, hoping to catch a last glimpse of Tiger, or Sam. I saw neither.

"Do you have relatives you can live with?" Jackson asked as the land receded.

"Nope. I'm the last of my line." Maybe I'd try to mend things with my sister eventually, but I wasn't ready. "I've got money though, at least the last time I checked."

"We'll set you up in a hotel until you get on your feet."

It was dusk as we approached the Golden Gate Coast Guard station. The bridge was lit up, waves of color moving up and down the spans. My breath caught in my throat. I'm not that old, really. I might have ten or even twenty more years of good life in me, even without organ replacements. That's a long time. I felt scared and excited.

Why was I leaving now, after fighting so hard to stay? Just being on the boat, near the crew, made me tremble with the relief of human proximity. I hadn't been that scared, but the loneliness had snuck up.

So Courtland was behind me. The water would keep rising. Sam and Lion would keep each other company, hopefully keep each other alive. Tiger would live out his remaining days feasting on mice and songbirds. My house would rot and fall.

Would my local apocalypse spread to the rest of planet? Too soon to say.

The hovercraft docked. Holding Jackson's arm for support, I stepped onto the pier. Someone handed me Rachel's rope. Someone else carried my bags.

Would my hotel accept goats?

Multa Ab Uno

by David England

"Madame President, it is over."

Chelsea looked up from the tersely-worded memo and into the deep-set eyes of her secretary of state. The older man's tightly curled snow-white hair contrasted sharply with the dark night of his skin, his face creased with years and responsibilities. A somber knowing hovered in the air between them. The general-turned-diplomat had been a friend of her family for decades, with a well-earned reputation for stating facts as he saw them regardless of the particulars of political winds. Although he'd have easily been able to rest on the considerable accomplishments of his earlier career, he'd acquiesced to being her first cabinet appointment in the wake of her history-making election five and a half years prior and had even agreed to stay on after her re-election.

Back before everything had come unglued.

She set the document down on the rich mahogany surface with a pointed deliberateness and let her gaze travel slowly down the length of the long meeting table, taking in the members of her cabinet. Compared to recent administrations, the group was significantly smaller thanks to the Executive Reorganization Act of 2027, which had reduced the number of executive departments from fifteen to ten: folding Veterans Affairs and Homeland Security into Defense, as well as pairing Agriculture with Interior, Education with Health and Human Services, and Labor with Commerce. What had been an attempt to demonstrate federal parsimony in difficult times had only served to swell the ranks of officials below that top tier. Senior deputy secretaries, deputy secretaries, undersecretaries, senior assistant secretaries, and assistant secretaries abounded. Rather like squeezing mud, she thought, the bloat merely oozed out between your fingers.

She had fought—oh, how she had fought—to attain this office, seeking to bring about the changes that needed doing. The public sparring had only been the visible tip of the proverbial iceberg and the backroom, intra-party combat had been close-quarters, bloody, and ruthless. Yet, despite it all, she had persevered. She had quelled the doubters and banished the shame that had become attached to the family name. Like any other politician worth her salt, there were elements of pride and personal ambition involved. One corner of her mouth quirked upwards by a fraction of an inch in rueful self-reflection: those who spoke of selfless leadership were either liars or fools, and in either case had never dealt with the reality of leading people.

But there had been something else, some deeper thing which had driven her as well. Deeper than redemption of the family, deeper than a desire to make her mark on history. Something that had hovered just at the edge of her awareness. An inchoate, elemental knowing that the nation had veered from its tracks and was hurtling unguided into dangerous terra incognita. It was that sense which had driven her to act, to cast her hat into the most vicious of political rings.

An amorphous, undefinable threat seemed to loom over the country. Others perceived it only vaguely, if at all, and even then only grasped at a sense that something was amiss. We were stumbling blindly, she had told herself in those moments before she announced her candidacy to an incredulous press those years ago. Despite all the nay-sayers, she had achieved success. At first.

"Two hundred fifty-seven years," she said carefully. "That is what the history texts will say: two hundred fifty-seven years, ten months, and eleven days. The length of the great American experiment." Her statement was swallowed by silence. An uncomfortable quiet lay over the room.

She'd begun her first administration with a relentless energy and focus, pulling a once-great nation back together again. Given it new pride and, she'd thought, new purpose. But all of those achievements had proven transitory and ephemeral. In the end, it had all come apart anyway, crumbling under the onslaught of the vast storm of forces battering the country. She had failed. She had failed the people of the nation, failed the voters who had put their faith in her, and failed the members of her cabinet who looked to her in this moment. Those eleven faces, some expressionless, some speaking all too clearly, regarded her now.

"No!" At the far end of the table, Carter Harris slapped his hand down hard on the polished surface. "This is not how it's going to end."

Chelsea considered her somewhat volatile vice president. Their pairing had been a calculated choice of political strategy rather than a selection from personal preference, his west coast clout serving to balance her east coast provenance and southerly Midwestern roots. Despite his being strongly opinionated and prone to rash action, the two of them had managed to work reasonably well together, at least in public. Of course, since their re-election, she'd noticed his focus increasingly geared toward supporting his own run for the presidency in 2036. An office which, in all probability, would no longer exist.

"What would you suggest, Carter?" she asked levelly. "Our forces are in retreat, our positions untenable. How long does one continue to fight a war that has already been lost? How many more lives must be destroyed by the fratricidal conflict?"

Harris glared at her. "This is the United fucking States of fucking America," he spat. "The most powerful nation on the planet. In history. We are *not* going down to a ragtag rebel army of state militia."

The secretary of state spoke up again, his tone carefully respectful, but pointed. "Mr. Vice President, our lines are broken."

"Bullshit," Harris replied forcefully. "We've got the Ohio River crossings under lock and key. We've held the Alliance to a standstill."

"A fact rendered irrelevant by the breakthrough on the West Virginia front," the secretary explained. "Anderson has our forces completely outflanked. We are out of options."

"There are always options," Harris retorted. "We just have to be willing to use them." He turned to the secretary of defense. "Am I right?"

The secretary shifted uncomfortably. "As you say, Mr. Vice President," he replied with a subtle emphasis on the first part of the title, "there are always options. We have resources yet."

"We may have resources at our disposal for the time being," Chelsea allowed. "What we don't have is the support of the people. Even if we were to win yet in the field, we have already lost this war."

"We have the support of the people who matter," Harris rejoined.

Chelsea ignored his response and cast her eyes over her cabinet. "As you may or may not be aware, I took a call from Geneva yesterday." No one needed to ask who had made that call. The city of Geneva had become synonymous with the United Nations when that international body had decided to relocate its headquarters in the aftermath of the 2020 US elections. "The secretary general has offered his services in mediating an armistice."

"Surrender, you mean," the vice president snapped. "You would permit the destruction of this country? Two and a half centuries of greatness? How can you even consider such a thing? And you call yourself an American."

Chelsea leaned in, her eyes hard. "This nation runs in my veins, Carter," she said, her voice dangerously calm. "My father was president of these United States and my mother should have been. I have spent my entire life in public service. There is no one at this table—no one—who is more dedicated to the welfare of the American people than I am." She sat back in her chair. "That's why I ran for this office in the first place."

"Then do what needs to be done," Harris challenged her. "You're the president of the United States, for fuck's sake. Act like it."

"Again, Carter, what would you suggest?"

"End this treasonous conflict," he answered. "Once and for all."

She quirked an eyebrow. "What is it you think I'm trying to do?"

"Not that way." Harris shook his head sharply. "The only reason these hillbillies have gotten as far as they have is because you've held back and refused to utilize all of the resources available. As we just discussed, we have other options."

Chelsea's eyes widened. "Carter, are you suggesting what I think you're suggesting?"

The vice president nodded, his expression stern. "Nuke the shit out of them. It's all fly-over country anyway. Not like anyone who matters lives there anymore."

"I cannot believe you would propose using our nuclear arsenal on American citizens and American territory." Her disbelief showed plainly. "Are you mad?"

"I would go to whatever lengths necessary and use whatever means available to preserve this great nation," Harris replied. "And I would deploy whatever weapons I had at my disposal against traitors who would seek our nation's destruction."

"There would be little of the nation left," the secretary of agriculture and interior commented dryly. "You would burn down the proverbial village in order to save it."

"We use tactical nukes." Harris waved one hand dismissively. "Limit the damage to the loyal parts of the country and concentrate the destruction where it belongs. Then we can rebuild afterwards." He planted his hands on the table. "We'd have a blank slate to work from, since the traitors have all identified themselves. Stomp on this thing hard, crush it, and then let's get on with making this country into what it should have been in the first place." A hard gaze held each secretary in turn. "We mop up and we push through the constitutional changes necessary to make sure this never happens again, that these people never have a shred of power with which to threaten this nation."

Chelsea stared at her vice president. How had it come to this? How had this nation come so thoroughly apart at the seams? Granted, she answered herself, we've been sliding down this slope for decades now, far longer than anyone has been willing to admit. The first manifestations of unrest, the first hints of something outside the norm, had been the sporadic urban troubles which predated even her one-term predecessor. Toledo had erupted in the spring of '24, with Birmingham following later that fall. Both had been dealt with, but like a malevolent rodent, the riots would disappear underground only to flare up again in some other city months later.

The previous administration had attempted the time-honored trick of rallying the nation around an external conflict and had subsequently intervened in Venezuela in order to remove from power a particularly troublesome dictator whose influence in South America had been attaining a status uncomfortable for American policymakers. Unfortunately, neither aim had been accomplished and her administration had inherited both a foreign quagmire and a simmering kettle of domestic unrest.

"Sixty-five years ago, this country put humans on the goddamn moon," Harris continued. "Five years ago, we went back. And two years ago, we established the first permanently manned lunar station. We've won two world wars, the Cold War, and kept peace around the globe. *That* is what this country represents. Progress. The conquest of space. Guardianship of the planet. The future of humanity." His eyes focused on her. "And *that* is what you are about to throw away to a bunch of rednecks."

Ah yes, Chelsea thought to herself. The revitalization of the moon program had been her own effort at sleight-of-hand, seizing on the beginning efforts of her predecessor's administration, rebranding the thing, and moving it to center stage. The Diana program had been the shiny object on which she'd sought to focus the public eye while she managed the Venezuelan debacle she'd inherited. Something to demonstrate the strength of the American spirit so that people wouldn't pay attention to the fact that their lives weren't improving any longer and were, in fact, steadily getting worse. Certainly, the installation of the first station crew in late October of 2032 had been a triumph of political stagecraft and all but sealed her reelection. Then the momentary glory faded and the wheels had come off.

Another flare of civil unrest, this time in Louisiana. Just like before, the National Guard troops were mobilized and sent in. But this time, the trouble wasn't in the urban centers, it was in the bayous. And this time, when the generals sent the troops in, the troops disappeared and didn't come back. The spin doctors did their work and painted the provocateurs as terrorists mercilessly slaughtering American soldiers, but she had known the truth. The soldiers hadn't been killed; they'd switched sides. The spin had limited effect and a brief shelf-life anyway, as the Idaho Guard units defecting to the resistance holed up in the Bitterroot Mountains had occurred in broad daylight in front of the world. The pockets of opposition got in touch with one another and got themselves organized. The facade was over and open rebellion had begun in earnest.

And that last crew of the lunar station. Dear God. If there were ever an executive decision that would haunt her for the rest of her days, it would be the choice to not bring the crew home while she'd had the chance. Her advisors, Carter at the forefront, had pushed her to keep to the schedule, to show no weakness as the sporadic violence had begun to coalesce. They might have applied the pressure, but in the end, it had been her call. And when the rapid cascade of events had cut off communication with the station, she had been able only to watch helplessly as the evacuation pod had attempted unguided re-entry through the lower-orbital debris fields and had exploded into a cloud of metal shards when it collided with a chunk of long-dead satellite.

The secretary of state cleared his throat, the sound bringing Chelsea's attention back to the present. "The Alliance forces are hardly rednecks, or hillbillies for that matter. These are National Guard units, Reserves, veterans' groups. Even some regular units have gone over."

"This government has lost the respect of the people," Chelsea stated, however reluctant she had been to admit that fact to herself. "We've lost the mandate of heaven."

"What the hell are you talking about?" Harris demanded.

"The mandate of heaven," Chelsea explained, "is a Chinese concept of political legitimacy." She didn't have a doctorate in international relations for nothing, she thought to herself wryly. "It was expounded by the Duke of Zhou at the outset of the Zhou dynasty, after the overthrow of the Shang in the mid-eleventh century BCE, describing how a just ruler might keep the favor of the gods but also how an unjust ruler might lose that mandate to another." She shook her head. "We've lost that legitimacy."

"You're insane," Harris retorted. "This isn't some university lecture hall. We aren't debating ancient mythology or oriental mysticism. This is about the future of Western civilization." He tapped the table's surface hard with a forefinger. "We're talking about whether or not this nation will continue to lead in the inevitable course of progress or collapse into a pathetic third-world backwater."

"The people seem to feel differently, Carter," she observed.

"As I said, those people don't matter. They're not worth the space they take up." He straightened. "I'm not going to stand by while a bunch of inbred hicks who don't know their proper place destroy the greatest nation on earth."

"I'm trying to save what I can of this nation, Carter," Chelsea pressed. "I called this meeting in order to discuss the secretary general's offer, but events have taken the decision from my hands. I'm going to accept." She pressed a button on the intercom.

"No, you're not," Harris stated flatly. "I'm invoking the Twenty-fifth Amendment right now."

"Yes, Madame President?" her assistant's voice came through the speaker.

"Claire," Chelsea said calmly, her eyes not breaking contact with Harris'. "I'm going to have to get back with you in a few minutes." Her hand moved away from the 'com. "What did you just say?"

"Don't pretend you didn't hear me," he responded, the disdain in his voice unmasked by any form of pretense. "I'm saying that you have demonstrated your lack of fitness for office and I am asking this cabinet's support for your removal."

"I heard you," she replied. "I just wanted the record clear." She stood, looking up and down the length of the meeting table. "Everyone—"

"No." Harris cut her off, standing as well. "No speeches, no arguments, no pleadings. We vote. Now." He looked at the faces of the cabinet. "On the charge of failure to execute her solemn duty, including the defense of this nation, and demonstrating her lack of fitness for the office of president, how say you?"

For a long moment that seemed to stretch forever, no one responded.

"Fine," The secretary of state said, his expression grim. "I'll start then. Nay."

The secretary of defense did not meet Chelsea's eyes, but looked at Harris. "Aye."

Transportation: "Aye."

Energy: "Aye."

Commerce and labor: "Nay."

Agriculture and interior: "Nay."

Treasury: "Aye."

Housing and urban development: "Nay."

Education, health, and human services: "Nay."

Justice: "Aye."

Harris smiled, triumphant. "And I vote 'aye.' That's six to five, Chelsea. I'll take things from here."

"Not so fast, Carter." Chelsea shook her head. A tight, humorless smile formed on her lips. "If you'd care to look, Section Four of the Twenty-fifth Amendment to the Constitution requires a majority of executive officers *and* the Vice President to declare a President incapable. You only have five votes out of ten. That is not a majority." She held her gaze steady, remembering that most important lesson she'd learned early in her political career: if you're going to make a stand, then make a stand. Never waver. Never let them smell blood. "The motion fails," she stated firmly, her tone emphatic, authoritative, and final.

"That's utter bullshit," Harris sputtered.

"Technically," the attorney general admitted with a shrug, "she's right, Carter."

"No," the vice president responded, incredulous. "God damn it, no! It is *not* ending this way." He reached for his waistband.

Time slowed to a crawl. Chelsea's awareness bifurcated, one aspect dispassionately observing the unfolding crisis even as her reflexes kicked into gear. So this is how it goes down, that objective voice commented. Shoot-out at the OK Corral. How typically American.

Ever since the Idaho incident those months ago, she had issued a confidential Presidential Memorandum permitting all executive officers to carry personal firearms for protection "in all places and locales at which the executive officer would have business." Not all had taken the opportunity to avail themselves of this protection and now, it appeared, her vice president was going to put that allowance to a different use.

Chelsea recognized Harris' movement as a draw from a concealed-carry holster because she had one herself. In one corner of her mind, she realized that she had seen the probability of this moment, that she'd known how he'd react when backed into a corner, and had been waiting for him to commit.

Like everything else he did, his movement was rash and sloppy, that coolly-detached portion of her brain observed. No staffer to clean up your jumbled mess this time, Carter, she thought grimly. No help with the turd-polishing here. It's all on you, baby.

The ivory-handled derringer was so small that it nestled in the palm of her slim hand. Aided by her instinctive response and the lighter weapon, the smooth action was bringing her pistol level before Harris' more cumbersome automatic had even cleared his holster. The vice president's eyes widened as understanding dawned as to what was about to happen.

Her derringer held a mere two rounds, but that capacity was twice what she required. Chelsea didn't hesitate, applying an even pressure to the trigger as the barrel came into line with her target. The pistol was only a .22, but it was more than enough to get the job done.

A red flower blossomed in the center of the vice president's forehead with a wet smacking sound and he stared at her in disbelief for the briefest of moments before his body slumped into the chair behind him like a marionette whose strings had suddenly been cut. The crack of her pistol echoed away into silence amid the frozen tableau of the room.

No one spoke. Somewhat anti-climatically, the Secret Service detail burst through the doors, weapons drawn. Chelsea calmly set her small pistol on the table, reached for the intercom, and pressed a button.

"Claire, please get me the secretary general."

Burning *Stardust*

by Matthew Spaur

When Suki climbed into Lewis's truck, she changed his plans for their first date. "I want to see that plane you showed me the other day," she said.

"It's usually out at the other airport," he said.

"Okay, let's go."

He drove north on Highway 2 out of Kalispell, puzzled and a little disappointed, heading towards Glacier Park International Airport.

In his rearview mirror he could see the laser light show over the Kalispell City Airport in his rearview mirror. That was where he had planned to take her. The smaller city airport hosted shows like that night's Fourth of July celebration, as well as Memorial Day and Labor Day because it was easier for people, meaning tourists, to see and attend. Kalispell was working harder to attract tourists since Glacier National Park's glaciers melted. The city's dark skies laws meant the nights above the Flathead Valley provided a purer matte canvas for laser and drone shows set to AI-improvised music. The waxing moon was still low in the east right now, which made an especially dark sky for the show.

Instead, Lewis and Suki cruised through the Rose Crossing intersection, with "Coming Soon" development signs posted on the right side of the road. Someone had spray painted a giant black X on one of the signs.

On the truck's bench seat between them lay Suki's backpack. It wasn't the hiking kind, or one of those vintage leather purse-looking ones with shoulder straps. Those might have made sense to Lewis for her to bring on a date. This was a student bag, the kind with drawstrings that formed the shoulder straps when pulled closed. The University of Montana seal was printed on one side, with "Suki" handwritten inside the university's seal. She wore very casual clothes for a date, too, more casual than he expected. He could tell she could dress up if she wanted and be a stunner, better than most. She was active and hiked and didn't eat junk.

He brought a backpack too, with padded shoulder straps and a few things he packed for what he thought would be their evening at the Independence Day Air Show and Drone Festival.

Before they reached Glacier Park International, she said, "Pull over—let's park here."

For a moment he thought, hoped, that she wanted to make out in the dark next to the empty road. Instead, she grabbed her bag and jumped out of the truck.

"Where are we going?"

"Show me that plane," she said, and closed the door.

He grabbed his backpack and followed her. They crossed the highway, two lanes at that point and still warm from the day's sun. They picked up a little speed descending the short slope at the far edge of the road, jump a small ditch at the bottom, and faced the chain link perimeter fence.

"Shouldn't we see if the gates are open?" Lewis asked.

Suki didn't answer. She pulled a flashlight from her bag, switched it on, and used the weak beam to search inside the bag.

Lewis couldn't believe he hadn't pack a flashlight for an evening date outdoors. He needed to get better at this dating thing.

She pulled a small pair of wire cutters from her bag and held them up in the light. The tool wasn't any bigger than a pair of pliers. "This is quicker." She snipped the bottom off one link in the fence. Then, with the flashlight, she traced the snipped link up about a meter, and snipped it again. She threaded the section out of the fence, leaving a one-meter vertical seam.

She pulled back one edge of the seam and gestured to Lewis. "After you."

They walked across the open field between highway and runway. Suki swept the flashlight side-to-side to help them avoid stepping in gopher holes. They didn't say much as they walked, a spot of light zigzagging through the dark field. In the distance he could hear the occasional pop and boom of fireworks, illegal for nearly 50 years now but still sold on the Flathead Indian reservation just south of town.

He felt sure Glacier International had some sort of security besides the fence. They couldn't be international without it. Probably sensors and cameras clustered around the hangars and buildings, tied to some online AI monitor. Good thing the airport didn't seem to have drones patrolling the fields areas, at least that he could see.

They transitioned from lumpy, scratchy field to the flat, warm runway. Suki turned off her flashlight. They followed the pavement north, continuing with Kalispell at their back. The first buildings they found were the smaller hangars for private planes and charter services, standing between the dark of the field and the bigger passenger terminals at the midpoint of the runways.

Lewis stopped Suki for a moment and scanned the four rows of planes parked in front of the hangar closest to the field. With so many planes, he guessed a lot of the digerati from the Van-SanFran corridor had flown in for the holiday weekend. There'd be a mix of autonomous and manual models here, biofuel and electric and hybrid, depending on how the rich liked their toys.

"There," Lewis whispered and pointed to the row of planes closest to the field. The one Suki wanted sat at the far end of the row nearest the edge of the parking area. They walked down the row. Lewis wanted to peek and gawk at each plane, but Suki made a straight line to the one he'd pointed out to her a few days ago.

"The propeller is in the back?" Suki said. "That's weird."

"It's a pusher prop," Lewis whispered. "That's what Grandpa calls it."

Suki stood near the nose of the craft and traced her finger over the script stenciling of the plane's name, *Stardust*. She could feel the bumps of glitter in the paint of the lettering. "I thought it would be shiny up close."

Lewis stood farther back along the craft. Up close this thing was sleeker, more high-tech, more beautiful than he imagined. He tapped its dark blue body with an index finger. "It's alloy. Strong. Light. Expensive, too." He tapped a window. "Polycarb." He touched two small hatch covers, one to each side of him. Both were about the size of a slice of bread. Both were locked. "It's a hybrid: plug-in and biofuel."

Last week Lewis and Suki were hanging out on her break from the touristy retail store across the street from the machine shop where he worked for his grandfather. He'd always worked summers and vacations in the shop, especially now that he was dropping out of the university. He noticed her a couple weeks earlier, leaning against the brick wall around the corner from the shop's front door. She looked like the girls at college, the ones he might not see again. Maybe she was a girl from college. He decided he better find out. And she was, except she said she was dropping out, too.

While they talked, a sleek private plane, midnight blue with big windows, flew over the two of them. Lewis told Suki about the guy who owned the plane, that he used to be a rocket designer for Taylor Aerospace and even trained to go to space but now flew tourists and hunters and miners and developers and rich people around Flathead and Glacier. Lewis was trying to impress her by sounding smart and connected. He said the pilot came in the shop occasionally for specialty parts that he couldn't find online and didn't have the equipment to machine or print himself, even though he clearly knew how. Grandpa said he'd bring in holographic blueprints of what he needed, very clean and precise work.

As Lewis talked, Suki shaded her eyes with her hands and watched the plane bank west, maybe heading towards the closest major airport in Spokane. "I wish developers and miners and loggers would stay away from here," she said. "I wish half the world was left wild. Maybe more." After the plane disappeared in the distance, she lowered her hands and turned to Lewis and smiled.

Lewis joined Suki at the back of the plane. "So why are we here, and where did you learn that fence trick?" he asked. He smiled nervously. "Are we going for a joyride? You're secretly a pilot?"

Suki pulled a small crowbar, maybe as long as her forearm, from her bag. Lewis's grandfather would call it a cat's paw. "Remember when you told me about what this guy does, flying hunters and developers and miners around? We're making sure that doesn't happen anymore."

"Why?" Lewis asked.

Suki stooped under one of *Stardust*'s wings, kneeled next to a tire, and held the cat's paw by the straight end. She swung the curved and notched end into the tire two, three, four times and more until it burst with a loud *POP*.

She crawled out from under the wing and stood up. "If we make it harder for them to hunt and build and pave and log and mine, they'll stop." She handed him the cat's paw. "Here—your turn."

Lewis took the tool. It felt surprisingly dense for its size. It still held warmth from Suki's grip. *Stardust* was a beautiful plane. Suki was a beautiful girl. He didn't know where any of this was headed.

He stepped to the nose of the plane, bent over, and drove the tool into the front tire. It burst on the first swing.

"Lucky hit," Suki said.

Lewis grinned for a moment. "Flat tires won't stop a plane for long."

Suki took back the tool and started wailing on the windows. The cat's paw made a dull thud, quieter than he expected, not a ringing sound like hitting glass. Quiet is good when you're vandalizing, he thought.

Nothing broke, nothing cracked. Suki carved a few scratches for her efforts. She dropped the tool—it clanged on the tarmac—then looked around and picked up a rock from the edge of the field. "Anything is a weapon if you use it the right way."

"Is that some slogan?" Lewis asked.

"Not sure where I heard that," she said. "Maybe my parents, but what would they know?"

She threw the rock straight and strong, like she had played a lot of ball, hardball not softball. Lewis had never played. The rock thumped against a passenger door and dropped to the ground.

"I told you about making half the earth wild again. Remember? There's this group, a cause, kind of. They don't have a name, but people call them Halfers. Instead of just talking about making half the world wild, they're doing it. That's what we're doing."

She picked up another rock and pitched it straight at a window. *Thump.*

Suki let out a growl. "Don't you see?" She picked up the cat's paw and started pounding on the plane again. "The glaciers and the fires and the floods and the droughts," she said, each thud punctuating her list. "Something needs to happen. People talk about it all the time, but they don't *do* anything."

She looked at Lewis. "I can't believe you didn't bring anything."

He pushed his eyebrows together. "You didn't tell me we were doing crime. I thought this was a date."

Even across the dark of night, she looked him in the eye. "If you knew, would you have come?"

He looked back. "Yes."

Suki gestured at his backpack. "So, what did you bring?"

He felt his cheeks flush. He opened his bag. "I thought we were going to the show." He pulled out a sweatshirt. "In case you got cold." A chocolate bar. "In case you got hungry." And two illegal fireworks—sparklers. "For us to share."

"You naughty boy."

"The reservation still sells them." He felt his cheeks flush again. "I forgot a lighter. I thought about that right when we turned north on Two." He looked at her. "We can come back another night, bring some tools from the shop, do this right."

"No. Nobody's around and the moon's still low. It's got to be tonight."

Lewis's brain kicked into intuition mode, something all the AIs and autonomous systems still couldn't replicate or replace. He spent enough time around his grandfather in the machine shop to learn how to think through a problem. *Stardust* wouldn't break. Maybe it would burn. The magnesium on a sparkler would burn longer and hotter than a match, if he could get it started. Fire needs fuel plus oxygen plus spark. The sparkler was fuel and the night air gave oxygen.

A solution flashed in his head.

He took the cat's paw from Suki. "Go find some long grass that hasn't totally dried out. The longer the better. And a couple rocks, kind of long and flat, about the same size."

Suki took out her flashlight again and pointed it into the field.

"Maybe up against the back of the hangar," Lewis suggested.

She turned to her left and headed towards the building.

Lewis pried open the door to the biofuel tank, which was on the pilot's side of the plane just forward of the pusher prop. Inside the door, he found just a screw cap sealing the neck of the tank. That was easy.

Next, he walked around the propeller to the other side of the plane to force open the engine compartment. He could see silver circles of both mechanical and encryption locks on the door to the engine compartment. Lewis slipped the tip of the cat's paw's curved end into the seam below the mechanical lock. Once the tool was firmly inserted, he started rocking forward and back, towards the plane and then away, slowly working on fatiguing whatever small metal parts made up the mechanical lock.

Suki returned just as his rocking was gaining momentum and Lewis was starting to breathe a little heavier than normal. "Should I leave you two alone?" she asked.

"Ha . . . very . . . funny," Lewis huffed and with a loud *POP* the mechanical lock gave way.

"Yay!" Suki said.

Lewis told her, "Not so fast." He used the straight end of the cat's paw to pry open the still-locked hatch as much as possible. "Hurry, wedge your flashlight in there."

"It won't fit."

Lewis put all his weight against the lever. "There, go, now."

"Still won't fit."

Lewis grunted. "Okay, anything."

Suki took her sweatshirt out of her backpack, waded it up, and stuffed it into the space Lewis was holding open.

He slowly shifted his weight off the lever. The compartment door pressed down on the ball of cloth but stayed open about five centimeters. "Good, that'll do."

He looked at Suki. "There's still the encryption lock, and it's probably got some sort of security uplink. Once we break that, we won't have a lot of time. Show me what you got."

Suki laid her two rocks and handful of grass stems on the pavement.

"Good work. Shine your light here."

Lewis used the broadest grass stem she brought to lash one of the rocks to the handle of the sparkler. When he was done, he held the sparkler by its tip and jiggled it up and down, to make sure the rock wouldn't drop off.

"What are you doing?"

"You'll see."

Next, he picked the longest, thinnest piece of grass she brought. He tied one end of the grass around the flammable shaft of the sparkler, about two-thirds down from the tip. At the other end of the grass stem he tied the second rock.

"Bring your light."

He walked back around to the fuel tank. He slid the weighted sparkler a little way into the neck of the tank and then held it with just the long piece of grass. He tugged on the long grass to test the pull of the weight. Then he let the rock on the long piece of grass just hang, without moving his hands more than a centimeter from the stem. The two rocks acted as counterweights and kept the sparkler in place in the neck of the tank.

He took the sparkler and rock assembly back out. He walked back around the propeller again to the engine compartment. Suki followed him with the light.

He laid the sparkler assembly on the ground under the plane. "Don't step on that," he told Suki. "Here, shine the light up here."

She pointed the light at the open crack of the engine cover.

Lewis held the cat's paw with two hands, one around the curl and one on the straight, and drove the tip of the metal rod into the slender opening of the engine hatch again and again, ramming the square casing of the encryption lock. "Dammit, break." He was huffing and grunting until the mounting screws for the lock gave way. The compartment hatch rose open with the lock mechanism still attached.

"We need to hurry."

Lewis traced circuits until he found what he thought was the ignition circuit. That would probably have power. He wrapped the cat's paw in Suki's sweatshirt as insulation and used the bar to pry up and break the wire.

"Hand me the flashlight," he said. Lewis rested it so it shone mostly on the broken wire. "Okay, grab the sparkler. Careful."

Suki picked up the sparkler while supporting the rocks and grass stems.

He guided her hands closer to the engine. "I need you to hold the sparkler, so it pins down one end of the wire, like this. When I touch the other wire to the sparkler, it should light. I'll get a little shock, but don't let that startle you. Got it?"

"Yes."

Suki leaned in and held the sparkler tip in the circle of light, pressing down on one end of the broken wire. Lewis picked up the loose end of wire and touched it to the sparkler.

"*Jesus H. Mother—*" Lewis swore and jerked his hand back.

The magnesium in the sparkler flashed to life with a burst of white light.

"It worked! Are you okay?"

"Here, give it to me."

She handed the delicate burning arrangement to him. Lewis and Suki walked around the propeller to the fuel tank. He slid the weighted end of the sparkler into the neck of the tank. Bits of hot sparkler dropped onto his wrist, burning his skin. Now that the sparkler was lit, he realized it might burn the grass stem earlier than he thought, before it reached the knot on the sparkler, because the grass was laying alongside the burning shaft in the neck of the fuel tank. He let the counterweight rock dangle, slowly withdrawing his hands until he was sure it would stay in place.

"Okay, go! Quick!" Lewis started running away from the hangar and towards the runway.

Suki ran around to the other side of *Stardust*.

"Where are you going?"

"Our stuff!"

Suki scooped up her sweatshirt and their two backpacks, took her flashlight from the engine compartment, and ran to catch up with Lewis.

They were three planes away from *Stardust*. Lewis turned and took shelter behind the fuselage of a white six-seater with red pinstripes. Suki followed him. From their hideout they could see the sparkler's brightness reflected on *Stardust*'s dark alloy skin.

"So, the sparkler burns through the grass, the one rock falls and the sparkler drops into the tank?" she asked.

"That's the plan."

"Genius." She kissed him—their first kiss.

They saw the plane swallow the sparkler's white brightness and before the sound of a stone hitting pavement reached them, the flash of the fuel explosion robbed them of their night vision.

A loud boom followed and then *Stardust* itself became a giant sparkler as the lithium in the plane's battery caught fire, shooting white jets of flame. It was their own fireworks show, like video of the old July 4th shows, before droughts and fire danger and razed neighborhoods drove a nationwide ban on fireworks and drone shows filled the skies with sterile, programmed cartoons of patriotism and nostalgia.

The burning lithium jets looked like they might catch other planes on fire.

"We gotta run," Lewis said. He stepped in the field, heading for the truck.

"Wait," Suki said.

She scurried up to the nose of *Stardust*, as close as she could get. From her backpack she pulled a can of fluorescent green spray paint. On the ground next to the popped front tire, she painted a green circle the diameter of a ponderosa pine trunk. With a flick of her wrist, she divided the circle in two with paint. Then she filled in one half of the circle with green.

Suki tossed the paint can onto the flames. Lewis heard a ping as it exploded.

They ran. Suki started off immediately over the field. Lewis called her onto the tarmac, so they could go faster on the flats, before cutting straight across the field of gopher holes. No one seemed to be chasing them, no security drones that they could see or hear.

This time, they forgot to use the flashlight. Lewis caught the toe of his shoe in a gopher hole and landed hard in his chest. He was up on his hands and knees, wheezing before Suki caught up with him.

She put her arms around his chest and helped him stand. "Are you alright?"

"Just the . . . wind . . . knocked out . . . of me."

She helped him start to walk again, then trot, then run the last few meters until they reached the fence.

"Where's our hole?" he said.

Suki swept the flashlight beam across the fence. Because their opening was just a slit, it blended into the rest of the fence.

Lewis grabbed the chain link and started shaking it. "Not here," he said. He moved to his right, past one pole, and shook the fence again. "Nope."

Suki moved one pole to the left and rattled the fence. "Not here."

Lewis moved another pole to the right. "Nothing."

"It's here!" Suki said.

Lewis ran to her and ducked through the opening. They jumped the ditch, lumbered up the short steep slope to the road, and crossed to the truck.

"Holy . . . Christ," Lewis huffed, "I didn't . . . think it . . . would work."

"Can you drive?" Suki asked.

Lewis nodded.

"Get in quick. Let's go. Kill the lights."

Lewis pulled back onto Highway 2, driving dark and heading north. They passed the silent main gates to Glacier Park International.

"Where to?" he asked.

"Turn right at Jellison."

At the north end of the airport, he turned right at Jellison Road. When he left the highway, he switched the headlights on again. Deer might be out, and he didn't want to hit one. The backroads ran due south, almost paralleling Highway 2.

She guided him from Jellison to Helena Flats to Bayou Road, until they came to a park on the banks of the Flathead River. As the raven flies, they were a short way east from the scene of their crime. If it wasn't for the summer's perpetual tinge of wildfire smoke in the air, they might have been able to smell the burning plane on the night breeze.

Lewis backed the truck down to the river's edge. The Flathead in summer was low, barely a whisper with no glacial melt and the feds trying to keep enough water in Hungry Horse Reservoir just east of them.

He flipped down the tailgate and spread out his sweatshirt on the cool metal for them to sit on. He took out his chocolate bar.

She pulled out her sweatshirt and put it on. From her pack she took a bioplastic tub of huckleberries and a bottle of water still warm from the day. They split the berries and chocolate between them and passed the water back and forth.

"Have you done anything like this before?" he asked.

"Little stuff," Suki said. "Pulling up survey stakes, slashing tractor tires. Nothing like tonight." She tossed a huckleberry in the air and caught it in her mouth. "That was amazing."

"If we make half the Earth wild, then what about the people who'd have to move or lose their jobs?"

"Screw the other half," Suki said. "People are already losing their homes and jobs and lives. I mean, my God, Whitefish burned to the ground not that long ago. Shouldn't all that pain at least be for a good cause?"

"So why now?"

"Nobody is doing anything big enough, fast enough. Someone needs to reverse course. My parents named me Sequoia for god's sakes, like that would help."

She stopped for a moment. "Please, don't tell anyone. I hate that name."

Lewis laughed. "I won't."

"You have to promise."

"I, Lewis Whitmore, promise to never reveal Suki's true name."

"Good. I mean, it's rare just to see a hummingbird anymore." Suki paused again. "My cousins died in the Whitefish fire."

"Really? I'm sorry."

"Both of them, sleeping over at a friend's house. Birthday party."

"That's awful."

"My aunt and uncle are still torn up. She started drinking, hard. They're probably getting a divorce."

"Geez, Suki. That's rough."

After a moment, Lewis asked, "Do you know any real Halfers?"

"No. My folks dragged me to a Half-Earth meeting once. That's an actual group, pushing for policies and voting and fundraising and all that crap. I like that Halfers don't have meetings. 'If you can't build, destroy.' That's what I've heard."

She took a long drink from the water bottle. "You're full of questions. What about you? What have you done?"

Lewis shook his head. "I boosted some low-tech stuff, tools and supplies I wanted back in junior high. But nothing real. Nothing with an agenda."

"So why did you do this tonight, with me?"

"To be with you."

"You can't be that desperate to get some."

Lewis laughed. "Not just that. I feel like I'm missing out. Intensity, excitement, a cause. It's hard to feel sometimes."

He slipped his hand around hers. "Grandpa taught me all the old-fashioned stuff like hunting and fishing and working on antique fuel motors. That didn't win me friends with the screenheads at school, but I love it. Now Hungry Horse is barely half full, and the fish are mostly gone. It's harder and harder to find snow to drive on in the winter. We have to haul gear nearly to Banff anymore. That's tough with Grandpa getting older and biofuel going up."

He stopped, shrugged his shoulders. "Things aren't heading in the right direction. Maybe it's time for me to get passionate about the things I want to keep."

Lewis let go of Suki's hand and took the second sparkler out of his backpack. "I still don't have a way to light this." He flicked his wrist and sent the metal stick twirling through the night and into the river.

"Why'd you do that?" Suki asked.

"Disposing of possibly incriminating evidence," Lewis said in a lawyerly tone.

"Oh, really."

"Think we can still make the drone show?" he asked. "It could be a decent alibi."

Good Time Boy

by Violet Bertelsen

Henry rolled over in bed, heart-racing, the taste of sediment in his throat as he remembered his dreams, shuddering. He was back at the mandatory minimum school in that rotting white classroom, where he presented an essay on the fungal associations between the roots of the black oak. While talking about the unknown thousands of mycorrhizal associations that the roots have, he said, "The roots are the place of residence of the soul of the tree; it is interesting to say the least that the ancients believed that the trees housed nymphs, feminine numina, that for whom the ancients in their wisdom left offerings . . ." As he said these words, his classmates, who had previously ignored him, hunched over their cracked and dirty screens like gargoyles, all looked up at him, their eye sockets blackened; as they touched their screens, staring at him with their ghoul's eyes, Henry's head was taken by a tremendous buzzing of the digital thoughts directed malevolently towards him. As he struggled against the dread vibration of evil his body began to convulse and he woke up, covered in sweat on his cot.

He sat up and drank from a glass of water that lay next to his bed. Taking his journal, he carefully noted the dream, and then put the notebook back on his milk-crate nightstand. His room was small, eight feet by five feet, but at least he had a little east-facing window which helped him to rouse with the dawn. Henry got out of bed. He sat down on his chair by the window to do his daily ritual and meditation, finishing with his prayers to Christ and Aphrodite Pandemos. After this, he changed into his work garments that he kept under his cot. Carefully now, putting on the hot pants and tank top over his long, lanky limbs and trying not to knock any of the books and papers that were so crammed on his little bookshelf. The books and papers he had managed to accumulate and salvage from his old life, before the drought came and things had gotten ugly for a few years. To the east was the window and the west was the door, which he exited.

The other good time boys and girls were getting up too and helping themselves to the breakfast that the Madame, Nitzah, so generously provided. This was a clean house, and so the prostitutes weren't tranqheads or hooked on rekt. Those who brought in drugs were asked to leave. No one had screenpads. Nitzah was a Hermetic Christian and wouldn't allow such things in her establishment. She managed the finances and clients the old fashioned way, with a book and calendar.

Henry entered the old cafeteria and sat down next to Natalie, who wore a rough cotton smock and weathered trousers. She was absorbed in a history book, but nonetheless Henry said, "Morning!"

"Morning," she said, taking her dark eyes off the book, her finger marking the line she was on, smiling warmly.

"May I ask, Natalie, what you're doing today?" asked Henry, cup of coffee in his hand.

"Hmmm," said Natalie. "I didn't have any plans except to read this book. What are you doing?"

"Going up North. I know some woods twenty miles from here where there are good herbs and edible plants; you said before that you were interested in learning more about herbs. My afternoon trick cancelled, so I'm free till midnight. In an hour and a half I'm going to get on the bus, and you are welcome to join if you don't have clients today."

Natalie looked nervous. "What about the screenheads, Henry? Nitzah told me that some Christians got murdered a few weeks ago?"

Henry nodded. "Christ will protect us, and so will the Guardian of the Forrest," he said, crossing himself.

Natalie crossed herself too and nodded once.. They finished eating and grabbed some bags and hit the bus.

They sat together on the bus, sweating in the brutal heat that was now, somehow, normal. Henry took the window seat in his cutoff jeans and tank top and baseball cap at a saucy angle, one of his long brown legs leaning against the seat in front, the other turned under. Natalie still read her book, sweat forming on her brow. Henry looked around the bus; everyone else seemed plastered to their screen, distracted, uneasy and upset, hunched over their screenpads. *This is what cities are like*, thought Henry, *filled to the brim with screenheads giving such a nasty vibe.* He frowned to himself. *But I should feel grateful; at least this isn't the 'burbs with the horror of the work gangs and the bloodtheft.* He shuddered at the memory of the stories some of his fellow prostitutes who'd escaped from the 'burbs had shared. *No,* he decided, *I'm grateful to be here, even if it is hard at times.* Both Henry and Natalie were Hermetic Christians that had taken the initiate's vow to never touch a screen.

"On the way back I need to remember to get some more paper," said Henry to himself.

"Okay," said Natalie, lifting her gaze. "Why?"

"Secret project," said Henry. "Top secret. I could tell you but then I'd have to kill you!"

"C'mon Henry! Don't be a bugger!" teased Natalie.

"Sorry, I would but I like you too much," teased Henry back, leaning in his seat and stretching his long arms up.

They reached their stop and got off. Natalie grabbed Henry's arm. "Did you see that man staring at us?" she asked, a note of fright in her voice.

"Nah," said Henry insouciantly.

"He looked angry! Really mad. His face was white, like there was no blood in it, and he pointed his screenpad's camera at us and took our picture. The thing that got me is he wore a really . . . malignant smile" she explained, her lips pulled down in fear.

Henry sighed, and held Natalie's shoulder with a brotherly touch. "That's just how it is, Nat. People get nervous around us because we don't use screens. People . . . don't make sense. Now with more and more people losing access to their screenpads, and the screenpads getting worse and worse, from what I hear, people seem like they're freaking out when others choose not to use them. People have staked their entire identities to their screens, for three generations. My sense is that lots of people hate us since we have our vows and . . . people hate God, praised be His Name. But . . . for what it's worth, I'm here, and I promise you Natalie that as long as I'm around I'll protect you the best I can." He paused. "But let's clear our auras and enter the mysteries of the forest. Let's do the clearing breath, exhaling our earthly fears and inhaling the bravery of Spirit."

They spent a few moments breathing deeply and reciting their prayers silently and then Natalie whispered, "Thanks, Henry."

For the next few hours they laughed and cut nettles, dandelion greens and chickweed. They dug up burdock roots with sticks and then did their best to wash off in a creek, thanking the plants with a little sprinkle of oatmeal.

On the return trip they carried bags of herbs and on the bus they sat quietly on the cracked plastic seats, in companionable silence and lost in their own gentle trains of thought. But with their dirt and their bags, all eyes were on them, and a deep hostility filled the bus slowly, like a smoldering fire.

A group of teenagers surrounded Henry and Natalie, laughing scornfully and jostling each other as they brandished their cracked, dirty and taped together screens at the two Hermetic Christians, showing videos of religious folks getting their heads bashed in with steel toed boots, being mauled by dogs, tortured with coat hangers and pruning shears. The teenagers maliciously laughed at the two in their seats.

One girl in the group said, "When you go against progress, progress goes against you!"

"Henry, this is the stop for the paper shop," said Natalie.

"Of course." Henry pulled the wire, broken and retied many times, to ring the bell by the driver. Thankfully it was working today. The bus stopped. The teenagers stood their ground, not giving them space to get off.

"This is our stop," said Henry, looking the teenagers in their faces as they avoided his gaze.

"We're not letting you leave," growled the girl, who was clearly the leader of the pack.

"Christ permits us to leave," said Henry with a grace and power not his own, and the teenagers looked nervous and frightened as he and Natalie got up from their seats, the air brighter around them than before.

"Just let them off!" screamed the bus driver suddenly, brandishing a ratty, busted up baseball bat, a dangerous look in his eyes. The teenagers gave Henry and Natalie enough leeway to get through the side door. The teenagers took pictures of the two prostitutes as they exited, and then made slit throat gestures with a hand under the chin through the windows as the bus left.

As they exited, the brightness in the air that seemed to surround Henry wore off, and Natalie lost the focus and grace that had just a moment ago filled her. She began to cry. "I'm so frightened. I don't have the strength of your faith. I'm scared that you or Nitzah would reject me. The whorehouse is all . . . that I have. My parents died in the Hemorrhagic fever of '22 and a few months later I took the vows and now . . . I do the prayers and feel no grace, but so much fear—horrible, animal fear."

"Natalie," said Henry tenderly, "what I feel towards you is nothing but compassion. For whatever it's worth, I got your back, me and the other Hermetic Christians and even cynical old Nitzah."

Natalie laughed in spite of herself. "Even Nitzah?"

"Yeah, come here; please let me give you a hug." They embraced and Henry kissed the top of her head. "I got your back, Natalie, but let's stop making a scene, eh? Let's get some paper and get out of here."

When they got back to Nitzah's house, Henry gave the nettles, chickweed and dandelion greens to the head cook before getting ready for his midnight client. The house ate well for the next three days.

Several days later Henry had the time to recommence his project. He was carefully copying Matthew Wood's *Earthwise Herbal Vol. II: New World Plants*. Three years ago he had purchased both volumes from a used bookstore he frequented before it had been burnt to the ground during the War. The first volume was in pretty good shape, but the one he copied had a disintegrated binding and if it wasn't copied there would be nothing left. Carefully he folded the eleven by seventeen inch sheets in half and then sewed them together; he ruled the lines in pencil and carefully copied the words with his father's fountain pen using good India ink. Henry wrote in clunky block letters, but they were at least very legible, if not elegant. The work brought him satisfaction. He found that when he was left with nothing to think about he started to think about how much he despised the earthliness of his body, how much he should like to shed it and live in spirit, and spirit alone, and how nice it would feel to let a razor blade open some arteries and leave his horrid earth body behind.

These shameful thoughts carried with them a certain morbid sexual desire, and if he followed them he would soon fantasize about men sexually using him like a woman, and that brought him strong arousal, but also guilt. The prayers, rituals, and meditation helped, but still he had to contend day in and day out with both his homosexuality and its aura of degradation and shame. The division was deep in his soul: How to worship both Christ and Aphrodite Pandemos? Henry would ask himself this, but was never quite able to find satisfactory reconciliation.

But when he simply sat and copied Matthew Wood's delightful prose, saving it for future generations, he felt something close to peace. Perhaps that was the resolution for his turmoil. At these time he felt his body as a luminous servant of his spirit, and he didn't have to contend with his *earthly and dirty* desires for death and sex, and so his mind relaxed and life seemed to assume a more sacred purpose.

Usually Henry saw three or four clients a day, busy workingmen who didn't have time to visit gay bars but still craved flesh. Most younger folks would just look at porn and content themselves with fantasies and a vibrator or mechanical vagina, or would enter erotic virtual reality or chat with a lovebot. It may have been a bit more expensive than meeting someone, but people are complex and have unsightly emotions and betrayals. The techno-love may have been missing something vital, but it was safe from emotions. Henry considered this in light of his own intense ambivalence. *Well, I may be torn*, he thought with a grim smile, *but at least I'm brave enough to experience something a little more real than a sexbot.*

Luckily for him and the other prostitutes, many folks still craved that vital something: the warmth of skin, the moisture of a mouth, the taste of semen, the beating heart next to theirs, and the mad rush of *feelings* messy and earthly and real. Nitzah had a good business.

That Tuesday, Henry and Natalie went to the little park by Nitzah's house. They picked linden flowers as surreptitiously as possible, placing them into their purses.

"The flowers are an exceptional nervine," explained Henry. "That is, they are re-laxing to the nerves. They're relaxant and sedative. They both relax tension and se-date heat. They help people who are grieving and help to open the possibilities of imagination. Also really good for helping people fall asleep. Diaphoretic too, so it can be useful to break a fever. Linden is also especially good for the heart. See the leaves? They are shaped like an anatomical heart, but with serrated edges, like it's trembling."

"I see it, Henry."

"Oh wow, next to it is the tulip poplar. Also a heart medicine, it's good for bro-ken hearts, remember?"

"Is that what you gave me after my good time boy left me for a screenhead?"

"Yeah, it's warming and relaxes tension. Good for the appetite, good for the heart."

Henry was caught up in his enthusiasm. He took in his hand a black cherry twig and, after a few mumbled words to the tree, broke it off. "This wild cherry is good for coughs that sound like someone clearing the throat, helps soothe digestion and good when there's too much autoimmune force. Here, Nat, smell it," he said, hand-ing her the twig.

Nat's eyes grew big. "It smells delicious!"

"The pine, smell the pine, it helps oxygen into the lungs. It kills germs power-fully; the pitch can be used to cover wounds and it really promotes healing and keeps them clean. It's good for dislodging stuck mucus, especially when it's green and thick and sticky. Care should be taken though; it can be hard on the kidneys."

"I love the trees, Henry. I don't know nearly as much about them as you do, but I love them just the same."

"They're lovable. Growing up they were my best friends, they have beautiful souls, especially the big ones. Oh! This one, let's cut a branch right quick. Okay Nat, sprinkle some oatmeal . . . okay, great." Henry snapped a branch. "This is sweet birch. It tastes minty and is full of minerals. It is the most relaxing tea, and you can just keep on boiling the same twigs forever. We'll have some going at the Good Time House, most people love it."

Now walking the three miles back, they tried to keep their packs of of herbs in-conspicuous. "It's more than just the uncertainty that saddens me, Nat, it's the knowing in my heart that bad things are going to happen," said Henry. "In my meditations, in my dreams, whenever I look forward I see dark times ahead."

"Me too, Henry. It's scary, but at least you have your faith."

Henry smiled. "That's true, they could take my body, but not my overwhelm-ing love for Christ."

Nat smiled too sadly. "It's strange, Henry, when I'm around you and your love of Christ, I feel it, I feel it powerfully, but alone I feel nothing."

Henry considered that. "Perhaps there is some other divinity you could pray to. I pray to Aphrodite every day as well."

Nat took that in. "Really? You don't feel it violates your vows?"

"Not at all. There are different levels of the self and everyone has different affinities."

Natalie frowned and grew thoughtful as they returned to Nitzah's house.

That night, Henry finished copying *Earthwise Herbal Vol. II: New World Plants*. He sewed it together as neatly as he could and then put on a leather covering cut from a jacket that a john had given him a few years ago and he never had worn once. *Now*, he wondered, *what am I going to do to fill my free time?*

A few months later a furious mob burned down the Good Time House. Henry got out with little more than an outfit, his three volumes of *Earthwise Herbal*, and a canteen. Natalie got out with her empty backpack and a glass cup. As they got out, they were pelted with stones. They were lucky to find each other in the shade of a linden tree in the park. Chaos was everywhere, and the mob was murdering those they caught stumbling from the black smoke. "Well, the future is here," said Henry.

Natalie cried stupidly, and Henry led her by the hand deeper into the park. They drank from the head of a stream there. "Now we got to try to find the Hermetic Christian safehouse, in the suburb to the north. Here," he said, giving Natalie his hand-copied manuscript wrapped lovingly in wax paper, "take this; I have another copy in my pack. I hope to Hannah that I don't need to do it again but take it in your purse. There, if only one of us makes it then at least one copy will make it . . ."

"Henry, I'm scared! Don't talk like that, please! What's going on?" Natalie was trembling and crying.

"Take this," said Henry, and gave her some linden flower tincture. She regained her composure. "There is organized violence against us—screenheads, I think. if we can make it to the safe house we might be okay, otherwise . . . I don't know. We might not both be able to make it, but perhaps one of us will. Please, just to humor me, take one of these manuscripts." Henry pressed the wrapped manuscript into Natalie's pale and trembling hands.

After looking at the package, which was so like a gift, Natalie said in a whisper, "You . . . knew that this would happen."

"Yes, I knew that our situation couldn't last long with the world falling apart and people needing to look for scapegoats. Natalie, you've been my best friend and . . . I love you like a sister. Please, I beg you, be strong."

With a shaky voice, she said, "I'll try," and put the book Henry had given her into her backpack.

That night they walked twenty miles to the north, towards the suburbs. The sky was overcast and heavy, it felt like rain. During the day they slept and ate berries. At night again they walked, going up a hill. Henry was about twenty feet ahead, walking so fast Natalie had to struggle to keep up.

As night fell, Natalie grew weary and fell further and further behind. She saw Henry stop suddenly and something told her to stop suddenly, as well. About fifty feet from him was a group of people milling about with torches, blocking the road and casting a malevolent glow. Henry walked toward them, but something inside Natalie forced her to dive into the underbrush. The crowd began to roar as one, as if possessed, and stones began to fall around Henry, some striking him in the chest and arms drawing blood. "I fear you not!" he screamed. Without looking at her, Henry walked towards his assailants, a gentle, comic smile on his face and his aura so bright, she had to blink as she watched him.

Natalie was now all alone in the brush, with hostile actors on all sides; she scurried deeper and deeper into the undergrowth. Lightning began to flash, thunder clapped, and a heavy rain fell down and the mob dispersed.

Natalie waited under a tree. Henry was dead, she knew that with an icy feeling in the pit of her stomach, but she felt that she could feel his presence around her, a certain brightness. And somehow, the tree or Henry or something, managed to keep her as the rain fell in sheets for many hours. As the rain stopped and the moon sank under the horizon, she continued north. The next day, Natalie, guided by the curious brightness that had protected her during the storm, reached the safe-house deep in the decayed suburbs, and there she made her new life. But that is, of course, another story.

TCHAIKOVSKY'S VOYEVODA, PLAYED ON FLUTE

BY LAWRENCE BUENTELLO

THERE WAS NO MUSIC ON THE DAY AFTER THE WORLD ENDED.

But today there *was* music, though it seemed so far away that the sound may have only been an illusion.

When Kirov first heard the sound, which initially seemed like the low whistling of the wind through the trees, he was sitting on the edge of the lifeless pond tying the fishing line around his finger. For the last few months all he'd heard was the wind, and then the chirping of insects, and animals returning, though very few, to the trees and empty buildings of the complex. He'd been casting into the pond for weeks, but hooking nothing except dead plants from the bottom. The fish that once swam in the pond's waters were dead; he'd seen their remains floating, then decomposing, but he cast his line nevertheless, hoping to be surprised. But there were no fish.

Kirov sat wondering if he was really hearing music, and couldn't decide whether to be excited or dismayed. The complex held nothing but electronic equipment, so reproducing electronic files was impossible, for words or for music. He longed for the antique technology, the mechanical technology that might allow him to find some entertainment from old plastic discs and hand-turned players, but nothing of the kind existed in the complex. The technology with which he lived relied on electricity, and there was no electricity; the portable generators also no longer functioned.

He stood at the edge of the pond, turning his head slightly toward the sound, or toward where he thought the sound originated, but just as he was beginning to believe he was hearing actual musical notes the sound ceased, and all he could hear was the rustling of the leaves.

He finally ascribed the sound to a species of bird with which he was unfamiliar, one that had only just returned from some distant region. Some of the birds had returned, and the insects, but from how far away? Perhaps from the other side of the planet.

He stared at the shimmering waters of the pond a moment, then slowly began unwinding the line from around his finger so he could toss the weighted hook one more time into the water.

Kirov couldn't conclusively verify that the world had ended, only the life forms in his immediate environment extending to perhaps a hundred miles. This was the distance he'd covered in the weeks after the event, having no intention of remaining in an installation populated by slowly decaying corpses. At first he thought some error had occurred, and the instruments the physicists had been using to bombard the subterranean modules had malfunctioned. But the further he traveled from the center of the installation, the more he became convinced that the deaths of the installation's staff, and the wildlife surrounding the complex, was the result of an actual airburst.

After his shock diminished, he estimated that the technology, and the threat of its use, had been phenomenally successful; and then he realized that the experimental units his team were testing had been successful as well, or else he would be dead. He searched the other modules, but the one he'd been occupying was the only one that had been in use at the moment of the attack. He was the only long-term test subject, and would have remained underground for another week if his equipment hadn't failed. He thought it was a technical issue, and climbed the long ladder to the surface to report the problem.

When the implications of the airburst became a disturbing equation in his mind, he fled the installation to search for the boundaries of the blast zone. The only functioning conveyance available was a bicycle, one that the couriers used to travel between modules, since all the electrical components of the other vehicles were effectively ruined, so he rode the bicycle as far as he could in a line from the center of the complex, but found only death. Sustained by the supplies he carried in a pack on his shoulders, he arrived at the nearest city, which was Helenka, and found the entire population lifeless.

Despite his military training, and the rigid psychology that had made him a durable test subject, he sat in this city of the dead and wept. After he got control of his emotions, he built a crystal radio from elementary parts, constructed a diaphragm from paper and foil to serve as a speaker, grounded the radio with pipes, built a satisfactory antenna, and listened for radio broadcasts. His uncle, Piotr, had shown him how to construct such a radio when he was a child, telling him stories of their use in the Great War. A primitive technology, but one he was certain would function. He remained in the city for three days, listening intently, patiently, and then ceased listening.

Kirov decided to go no further. The city itself was dead, all electronic devices ruined, and the promise of finding more people in the next city improbable. If no one was communicating within reception of his radio, then he'd have to travel untold miles with only a faint hope of finding other survivors.

He found new supplies, exercised his choice of a more efficient and comfortable bicycle, and began the long journey back to the installation.

The city might soon be overrun by disease—he had some doubt that viruses and bacteria were as vulnerable to the airbursts as complex life forms. Nature was fully capable of recovering from natural and man-made disasters. The installation was fully capable of sustaining his needs for years; policing its relatively few bodies would be far easier than trying to protect himself from the contagion of an entire city full of corpses.

When he returned to the complex he felt he'd made a mistake in giving up so easily, but he was weary, and only wanted to rest. Perhaps he would try again, but night after night of listening to his makeshift radio, and hearing absolutely no signals, kept him from making definitive plans.

After a few weeks, he stopped monitoring the radio.

Kirov heard the music again a week later—and this time, when he gazed up from the book he'd been reading—which was only a technical manual, and useless, since the technology it described would never be functional again—he heard it clearly, though as from a great distance.

He closed the book and held it across his legs. He sat very still and listened, and then closed his eyes and listened again; from very far away it seemed as if someone was playing music. The sound seemed to come not from a speaker, but from an actual musical instrument. He opened his eyes to the sunlight flashing through the leaves of the tree under which he sat, and for the first time in months his heart beat faster, though he was uncertain. Then the music stopped, and he rose from the ground and leaned against the tree. A few more notes seemed to play through the air, but he lost the sound when the book slipped from his fingers.

Kirov forgot the book and moved away from the tree, though he had no idea which direction might lead him closer to the music. Then he realized the music had stopped, but he stood for another few minutes listening.

This was not an illusion, surely not; he'd heard the notes clearly.

But it was impossible. No one could be alive anywhere nearby. He'd examined the grounds in a two mile sweep around the perimeter of the complex—surely he couldn't hear an instrument playing from more than two miles away. In the previous weeks, while he listened intently to the radio he'd constructed, he also scanned the sky above the complex for aircraft, aircraft of any nation, but hadn't seen or heard a single plane or jet. If some infrastructure remained, surely he'd see or hear someone flying overhead. But there were no aircraft, no ground cars, no vehicles of any kind, except for his ridiculous bicycle.

He must be hearing things; but he was almost certain—

I'm going insane, he thought, it's been too long—

Or *someone* was playing a flute—

The effects of electromagnetic pulses were known since the first nuclear weapons were used after the Second World War.

Further testing, especially atmospheric nuclear weapons testing, offered scientists fascinating studies of gamma radiation, and other energy effects, on electronic devices. Depending on its intensity and altitude, an atmospheric nuclear explosion could destroy or damage electrical devices within very large areas. Solar astronomers had earlier discovered that high energy pulses from the sun could have similar damaging effects. But while no one could do anything to deflect solar energy bursts, human beings *could* cease nuclear testing in the atmosphere, if only to prevent radioactive elements from raining down onto the environment.

Though the atmospheric nuclear testing ceased, the use of electromagnetic pulse weaponry did not.

The effect could be produced through non-nuclear technology, but these weapons were of a localized range. Other technologies were always being explored, including those that would destroy the electronic infrastructure of cities without destroying the cities themselves; but these were not secret technologies.

The secret technologies being studied, even as Kirov's world suddenly found its terminus, included Electromagnetic Pulse weapons directed at interrupting the bio-electrical processes of living organisms, both locally and on a massive scale.

Kirov had volunteered as a test subject, because the weapons were simply too sophisticated, and defenses for them had to be engineered. He and the other volunteers routinely sealed themselves into test modules and endured localized bombardment of high-energy EMP blasts. Later, their neurological processes were evaluated and recorded. Injuries were common, and one unfortunate death let all the volunteers know that theirs was a highly dangerous assignment. It was the height of irony that Kirov's participation in a potentially deadly series of experiments had spared his life.

The complex was large, staffed by many hundreds of people, because the threat of using such devices had become very serious. A weapon that could destroy millions of people, and their supporting electronic infrastructure, without harming the viability of the earth beneath their feet, was the perfect weapon.

Someone had decided that the time was right to use it while Kirov was situated in his protective module; perhaps his countrymen had retaliated. Who actually began this war was unknown to him. The Americans, most likely, but perhaps also the Chinese. But what did it matter? Those around him were dead, the only machinery available for his use was mechanical, and the simple child's radio he'd constructed from wire and strips of metal represented the most complex technology available.

It was inevitable—the past decade had seen a rapid decline in available environmental resources, not only locally, but world-wide. Famines had devastated the populations of underdeveloped countries. Civil unrest threatened the stability of the developed ones. Political ideologies were useless in a world of people fearing for their survival, and such desperation, combined with sophisticated technology, rewrote the equations for human civility. In humanity's past, wars were fought for conquest; but this war, if it could accurately be called a war, had been fought for bread alone.

Ideologies were legion—all animals competed for the same resources.

At the core of humanity lay a reptile's brain.

Kirov sat staring up at the stars.

A pair of binoculars lay in his lap, waiting for the moment he spied an aircraft, or a distant satellite. Light pollution from the cities was no longer a problem for stargazers. The sky, free of clouds, shone brilliantly with stars, more stars than his limited knowledge of astronomy could identify. Beneath the stars, on this cool evening free of sounds, he felt the beauty of the world briefly invade his mind, moving in and away from him as other memories competed for his attention.

He'd always loved technology. He'd attended the Technicum, at his father's insistence, because he showed an aptitude, and the promise of secure employment was important to the family. Technology was beautiful then, an ever-increasing expression of scientific principles manifested in machines. He might have been satisfied to remain a simple worker, but his aptitude was marked and, after training, he began his career with the Aerospace Defence Forces. His training limited him to support roles, but when the EMP project began he volunteered his services. An exemplary service record provided him the pathway to the security of the module when the airburst occurred—circumstances that were decided by purely practical considerations. He was a dedicated soldier, nothing more.

When he was a child, though—when he was a child his mother had taken him to a performance of the Bolshoi ballet, and he was entranced by the ethereal beauty of the dancers. He fantasized about becoming a *danseur*, of studying dance in Moscow, but he wasn't gifted, and had to keep his fantasies subdued. Still, the ballet led him to the classical Russian composers, and the other European composers when he had thoroughly studied his countrymen. In his module at the complex he'd listened to Tchaikovsky every day, until his earphones went silent.

As he watched the stars, waiting for the moon to rise, he wished that he'd been a dancer, or a musician, or an artisan that had created some experience, some artifact worth remembering. But he was only a soldier.

When the music began again he scarcely noticed, though when he became aware of the lilting notes he immediately lost all thoughts of himself.

He straightened, moved the binoculars before his eyes and began scanning the horizon.

With the moon still down, he only saw shadows.

But the music still played, more distinctly now because the winds were calm and the birds were quiet in their trees.

He listened while trying not to breathe, he listened patiently, and tried to interpret the melody.

A flute owns a special sound, less somber than a stringed instrument, less stately than a drum; though he had heard excellent musicians bending their instruments to sorrowful compositions, the flute alone conveyed the happiness of life, the piping, eternal joy incapable of being replicated by other instruments. A sprite or fairy dancing on a stage was only properly encouraged by a piping flute, an innocent sound, the note of new birth and endless potential. No drum beat for life, except for when a dirge was played in war. No string was struck except to sound the loss of innocence.

He dropped the binoculars in the grass. He listened, but couldn't identify the composition. Still, he heard the notes rising in the air, distant, yet clearly present.

After a moment he cupped his hands to his mouth.

"I am here!" he shouted, breaking all protocol. "I am here! I am Ilya Kirov! Where are you? Where!"

He listened for a response, but none came. The music continued, though he could only sense its general direction, and after a while the music ceased. If he had run toward where he thought the music had come from, he might have run a hundred miles, blindly, into darkness and the dead world.

He wanted to run; he wanted to leave the complex, but he was afraid he was hallucinating, that there was no music, for why should music come when he sat thinking of music?

Or perhaps he was only thinking of music because he'd heard the music before—

Kirov held his face in his hands, though he didn't cry.

He was lonely. He had to admit it, he was lonely for a world that no longer existed.

‡‡

Kirov carefully packed a knapsack with dry foods, water, maps, and a compass, intending to leave the complex. He included a handgun and several rounds of ammunition, though he wondered if the only adversaries he might have to defend himself against were phantoms.

But he didn't leave the complex.

He was a soldier, and trained to assess his status before acting.

Since his immediate command was dead, he would have to serve as his own officer.

All alone in the huge dining hall that used to serve hundreds of people, he sat at a long table with his hands folded and his eyes fixed.

If the world was gone, if humanity was only a fragment of itself, then he would be walking into a devastated world. If some portion of humanity remained he might find it; though if it lay hundreds or even thousands of miles away, he wouldn't, and he would have to find some way to survive alone. And if the enemy, if the nation that had done this to his beautiful Russia, were slowly moving an occupying force through the country he might find them, too, and engage them, or surrender. *Would* he surrender? A loyal son of Russia? Did Russia even exist any longer? The military forces? Was he even a soldier?

These were questions that had no answers in the empty dining hall. The answers lay beyond the complex, and finding them meant sacrificing his resources and potentially facing death.

He sighed, ran his hands through his hair, which had never grown so long in his life, and cursed the results of his analysis.

Another week passed, during which he paced the grounds like a zoo animal confined to an exhibit. He felt he had nowhere to go.

Kirov decided to revisit the experimental module.

He left the hatch unsealed as he climbed down into darkness, feeling as if he were descending into Hades for a conversation with the dead.

He had no problem finding his way in the dark, and sat in the command chair where he'd waited to see if the controlled bombardments would penetrate the shielding of the module. The reason why a man would voluntarily risk his life to improve the numbers of a scientific experiment eluded him in the darkness, though the concept must have made great sense to him in the days preceding the airburst. At that time he felt as if he were part of something greater than the life of a single human being; he felt as if his participation represented everything noble and meaningful about Russia, the Russian people, and the ideologies that had kept his society viable for hundreds of years.

But now he only felt alone, as if every physical manifestation of that concept lay in ruins.

For the first time in his life he couldn't reconcile the equations of society, or find value in human endeavors. A man had to be strong in order to survive, just as a nation had to be strong in order to endure; such strength depended on the willingness of both to endure great hardships, and great deprivations. Both had to be willing to suffer the consequences of war, killing, devastation. The ends justified the means—if Russia survived, and the Russian people, then any measure to ensure that survival was justified.

The only problem with this concept was that every other man and every other nation on Earth felt identically, and each justified the pursuit of war and devastation with an identical argument. The end of the argument was the use of the perfect weapon in pursuit of supremacy.

When Kirov thought of the artistic preoccupations of his childhood, of the splendor of music, of the dancers spinning across the stage, he wondered how a species could hold both the beauty of artistic creation and the creation of monumental weapons of destruction in the same regard; both were creations of the human mind, but while one enriched the species the other decimated it, if not completely destroyed it. What was the purpose of building a military machine so potent that it destroyed everything beautiful born of humanity?

Humanity had labored diligently to produce a weapon so powerful that it annihilated whole populations, so efficient that it crippled every defensive threat, so that when it was used no retaliation was possible.

Human creativity was being used to destroy creation, as in the myth of the Ouroboros, the serpent eating its own tail, preparing the world for the creation of new life by destroying the old. Or perhaps this was the Earth's best method for cleansing itself of a destructive parasite. And all the beauty that ever escaped from the depths of a musical instrument must be forgotten in the fulfillment of the natural contract.

Kirov suddenly felt an overwhelming claustrophobia—the thought of sitting in the small module far beneath the ground terrified him. He'd never suffered claustrophobia before, he never thought it was possible—but now he only felt the need to escape the darkness, to flee the module before the hatch above the tunnel closed on him forever.

He stumbled in the darkness, colliding with invisible instruments as he desperately clutched at the ladder. He climbed quickly, almost losing his grip in his haste, before finally entering the light again.

As he kneeled in the sunlight, breathing heavily, he realized that he was no longer a soldier, no longer a man with a mission. He was nothing, nothing at all—

‡‡

He found some paper and a pen and wrote a letter to his mother and father, and to his sister, telling them how much he loved them, and how he wished they could be together again. He hoped they were still alive, that they hadn't been touched by the attack. Then he wrote of holidays they'd spent together, of the places they'd seen, the celebrations, the marriages of friends, the meals they used to eat together in the small apartment.

When he felt the tears begin to form in the corners of his eyes he stopped writing, and forced the tears away.

Then he began writing another letter, a request to his commanding officer for reassignment. Of course, there was no one to deliver the letter, or read it, or act to grant or deny the request. The act of writing the letter was only a formality. Since he had no way of posting these letters, he left them on the table by the pen, and walked away from them, as a man might walk away from a failed marriage, or a ruined career.

And still he felt haunted by a lifetime of indoctrination in the political and social philosophies that had defined his every thought, belief, and action.

What were his responsibilities? What was his responsibility to a society that no longer existed?

Five days passed before Kirov heard the music again.

For five days he'd spent his time sitting on the crest of a hill, listening.

Now the flute once again played lilting notes in the air, and for the first time in many weeks he smiled, and felt a minor note of hope rising in his heart. He was certain now, certain that it was a Tchaikovsky composition, though he couldn't name the opus. The flutist played with determination, the instrument laughed brightly in the air, teasing Kirov with the possibilities.

If it was illusion, or if it was reality, it was the same to him; prior to the airburst, the structure of his life had been formed by his society, by his country, by his family, by his training, and by his service. Kirov stood defined by a hundred ideologies, and now those ideologies were as dead as all the people in Helenka, as dead as the personnel of the complex, or all the birds, beasts, and insects that had lived in this world ignorant of the species that had condemned them as collateral damage.

This music, this music coming from someplace real or unreal, was the only beautiful thing left in the world, in *his* world, which had been left to him as a terrible inheritance.

"I am Ilya Kirov!" he shouted, waving his arms desperately. "I am here! I hear your music! I hear you!"

He laughed then, but not deliriously, only happily, because he had finally moved away from the world that had abandoned him.

He ran to where he'd left the knapsack and slung it over his shoulder, straining to hear the music as it played, and then he hurried from the complex, no longer a soldier, no longer a son of Russia, no longer a partisan. He would find the music, and the musician, and they would dance together, and laugh, and discuss the way the world used to be; they would make a different world together, and live with that beauty only.

Kirov ran through the grass, over the hill, and beyond the tall fences of the complex. He ran, and as he ran he was certain the music was growing louder, more distinct. He was no longer a soldier, or bound by terminal ideologies.

He was free.

Scuttle Star Island
by Clint Spivey

THE HULKS WERE GROANING. In the predawn twilight, Isa could see the massive, beached container ships shuddering against the waves.

The storm had passed, leaving a clear sky twinkling with a few stars, but the heavy seas remained. The only interruption to the shrieking, rusted hulls were the crashing waves. Isa's gaze lingered on the brightening horizon between the towering ships for a few moments more before returning to her shoreline forage.

Isa was glad her weekly collection duty had coincided with the storm. The leisurely morning strolls were much preferable to her upcoming week working compost. Storms always left things on the beach. And while most of it was trash, there were often items for salvage. Already several lengths of rope and nets hung from her belt for later restoration.

Picking her way through the rocks and sand, she spied true treasure. Bracing for disappointment, she hurried toward the semi-circle protruding from the sand. On an island long since devoid of electricity or power, Isa clung to this one bit of personal fun. Kneeling down, she lifted the disc from the sand with care, lest she damage it.

She need not have bothered. The sand-dollar—a fine specimen with two holes at the top of the star—was broken nearly in half, its bottom portion nowhere to be seen. In all her twenty-four years on Scuttle Star, she'd not once found one intact. This would join the other broken pieces on the looped hempen twine back in her room, waiting one day for a complete specimen to complete her decoration.

The massive ships standing above the only witness to her dashed hopes, Isa returned to her work.

That's when she saw the ship on the horizon.

‡‡

The plan had been bold. Acquire as many old bulk-container ships as possible —easily purchased in a cratering world economy—fill them with topsoil, and scuttle them on the shallow shores of a distant island. Crewed with as many per-maculturists, soil specialists, botanists and assorted other trades, the isolated homestead of Scuttle Star had been born deep in the Pacific.

Isabelle had been one of the first children born on Scuttle Star. Her only knowledge of the world outside were the stories passed on by the Mothers and men. She'd learned of the world's terrible wars, fought over dwindling resources and climate-induced migration. But she'd never seen anything of the outside world other than what had either been brought or washed up on their shores. Now, staring at the mammoth vessel through her binoculars, she knew the outside world had found *them.*

She needed to tell the Mothers. Isa had been foraging on Scuttle Star's wind-ward side, where often the best flotsam was to be found. The group of ships known as Arbor were the nearest. That meant Mother Mahise. It was still early, but she might be awake. Isa scrambled over the rocky shore to the nearest bamboo and rope ladder and climbed the dozen meters to board the rusted ship.

Arbor was Isa's favorite of the many garden-ships. Even with the storm, there was only scattered damage, a few fallen limbs and fruit, but mostly leaves blown free. She jogged between the cool, shaded rows scanning for Mother Mahise. She'd passed through the apples and was nearing the citrus when she saw her. Curly black hair kept short, she was lean and fit despite her fifty years. Isa often wondered on her beauty those twenty-plus years prior when they'd first arrived.

"Did you see?" Isa blurted through heaving breaths as she approached.

"See what?" she said, not looking from her work binding a half-broken limb.

"The ship."

This halted her. She paused for a moment, her eyes closed before she stood. "Where?"

They moved toward what had once been the bridge-castle, climbing rusted metal stairs from the soilbed toward the remaining superstructure. Like its dozens of sisters strewn about the island, the rusted hulk had been gutted of anything use-ful. Wind whistled through glassless windows as they climbed. They exited onto the port bridgewing. All of Scuttle Star lie beneath them, from Arbor's boughs beneath, to the neighboring Herbal and Vineyard ships beside them. Mount Solemn rose from the center, the ancient volcano protecting the more delicate crops in its leeward side.

Mother Mahise was silent as she peered through Isa's binoculars. Isa had never known Mahise to blanch, but when she spoke, Isa heard the fear.

"Get to Onyxhall," she whispered. "Ring the bell."

‡‡

From the beach sands through the island's native palms, Isa hurried to Onyxhall. The storm had meant fitful sleep for everyone, but island life didn't wait. Many stirred with sunrise. Isa mentioned the ship to the few Mothers and men she passed, but didn't linger. She reached the clearing at Mount Solemn's base, once again out of breath, and hurried into the hall.

Built against the foot of the mountain, Onxyhall had been so named for its scorched appearance. Its timbers seared black, the charred wood kept the moisture and insects at bay. Within were kept the priceless treasures preserved from the world beyond the sea. Isa ran past the crowded bookshelves lining the walls, their delicate pages protected from moisture by the blackened timbers.

Sala was at the rear of the hall, tending to the weather gear that had been used in the days prior to the storm. All clockwork and coiled springs, they were the brassbound wonders of the world beyond.

"Hey, Isa," he said, with his usual half-smile. They'd brought enough doctors along to treat injuries and illness as best they could. But against teeth grown crooked, Scuttle Star offered no hope. Sala had an overbite that he hid with constant bowed head and sideways glances. Despite his lean, muscular body and not unattractive face, he always hid his mouth. He bent over the marine-barograph where he carefully removed the hempen sheet they used to record pressure tendencies. The massive dip in the ink before the approaching storm had given way to the normal rise in pressure after its passage.

"There's a ship," she said, moving past him. "Mother Mahise said to ring the bell."

Like Mahise, the mention of a ship got Sala's attention. "Really? What kind. Did you see people aboard?"

She paused for a moment, looking him in the eye while shaking her head. "It's giant. I didn't see people. But I saw something else."

Sala's eyes went wide. Like Isa, he'd been born on Scuttle Star. The fabled outside world, despite the Mothers' warnings of its barbarism, was something all the children wondered about.

"What did you see?"

"I'm not sure. But it was flat. And on top was an airplane. And, I think, a helicopter." The two stared at each other for a moment before she remembered her task, and hurried to the bell tower.

Onyxhall fronted a natural cave system beneath Mount Solemn. The thick hempen rope dangling from the rooftop bell hung before the doors to the caves. One of the doors was open where Sala had been stowing the weather gear. Within the dim caves she saw the many sacks of grains and rice from their bountiful harvests. Beyond were baskets of dried fruits, peppers, herbs and nuts. With their small population they'd never known hunger.

But with the arrival of outsiders, hunger might be the least of their worries.

Leaping as high as she could muster, Isa yanked the bell to life.

Onyxhall was full. All the island sat or stood beneath its scorched timbers, save for a few lookouts keeping watch of their visitors. Isa sat on the floor with some of the other youngsters. Outside of a feast she'd never seen Onyxhall so crowded.

Meyer, one of the original captains who'd beached his ship on the shores, had described the visiting ship. A single word had sent a chill through the room.

Americans.

"And what kind of aircraft?" Mother Mahise asked, her knobby hands clutched together on the table before her. Beside her sat the eldest of the Mothers.

Meyer shrugged from his own seat beside the men against the many book-shelves lining the wall. "Does it matter? Helo's got guns and rockets. Enough to pick us to pieces should they choose." The Canadian scratched his beard before continuing. "The plane looks to be one of those stealth jobs the Americans had. The kind that can take off vertically. Didn't see any missiles or bombs. But I think those were held inside."

"Nothing's launched yet." Everyone turned to listen to Pierrecin. His sonorous voice mixed with his Hatian accent always commanded attention. "But that doesn't mean they're not watching. Could be drones we haven't spotted. Might be watching by satellite."

"What could they want?" Mother Lang, the Brit once from Birmingham asked from further up the table.

"Does it matter?" Isa said, standing. "They're Americans. Whatever they want they'll simply take it."

Many of the Mothers and men looked annoyed at the interruption but let her continue. As first born on the island some twenty-four years prior, she occupied a unique position. Elder sister to all those that had come after her. A grown woman to the adults' reluctant acceptance.

"They'll do what you've told us so many times they did. Kill. Burn. Take. No matter how many times you've taught us of the outside world, it always turns to the same tale. The Americans warred *everywhere* over *everything*. And now they're here. To take all this."

Isa and the other children's education extended beyond the knowledge and skills required to keep Scuttle Star productive. She knew of world geography and history. The Mothers and men made no effort to hide the crumbling failures that had sent them all fleeing to Scuttle Star.

"Maybe they got to the founders," Meyer said. "Made them give up our location. Could be why they never made it here. Wouldn't take much waterboarding I imagine."

Isa wasn't sure what a waterboard was, but the grave looks it conjured told her enough. The only mystery greater than the Scuttle Star's anonymous founders was that they'd never arrived.

Isa had just readied another rebuke against the Americans when Sala burst inside.

"They've sent a boat."

Isa accompanied the small party meeting the Americans. On the rocky sands between two of Orchard's ships, they watched the approaching boat.

"I only see two," Pierrecin said.

Mother Mahise was beside him, as was Meyer. Others hid in the abandoned bridges of the ships around them, their ancient rifles at the ready if things went bad.

"Why don't they fly?" Isa asked.

No one answered. Only the waves filled the silence, echoing against the towering steel sides of the two beached ships. Soon, the roar of the motorboat reached them.

"Ahoy!" a smiling young man with a shaved head shouted while waving. The other man driving the boat seemed focused on keeping from being dashed against the ships. The two wore identical uniforms. Blue and gray digital camouflage tunics and trousers.

"Quite a place you've got here," the man said as the boat crunched to shore.

"I'm Mahise." She introduced the others.

"Bishop," he said, pointing to his nametape. "That's Weston." He pointed to his stone-still companion. He wore mirrored sun-glasses that hid his eyes. Isa saw his knuckles were white with how hard he gripped the steering wheel.

"This all of you?" Bishop asked.

"This all of *you*?" answered Pierrecin.

And on it went. Much spoken with little being said as each side tried to size up the other. Despite the smiles Isa noticed how tense the two seemed. The man in the boat trembled while the one speaking seemed to sway unsteadily. Had it been the many months at sea? Or were they eager to begin their conquest? Isa knew the answer to that. They were Americans, after all.

"Well," Bishop said during a lull in the conversation. "Didn't want to just drop by unannounced with the whole crew."

"Why didn't you fly?" Mother Mahise asked.

"Ah. Well, you know. Saving fuel and all. We'll probably warm the old bird up if you guys invite us back."

Invite us? The others seemed as perplexed by this phrasing as Isa. More lies to comfort them prior to an attack. It had to be.

"But we wanted to leave you something," Bishop said, turning toward the boat. He retrieved a battered old radio and handed it to Mother Mahise. "If you guys want to talk. Or need anything, give us a ring." He demonstrated which channel and frequency they were monitoring. She handed it to Pierrecin, who held it as if it concealed a bomb.

"Thank you," she said. "We'll be in touch. Perhaps we can get together again."

"We'd like that," Bishop said, climbing aboard the boat. He waved, smiling once more, and departed. The residents of Scuttle Star stood in silence as they motored away. Isa turned to speak.

Mahise silenced her with a quick shake of the head. Pierrecin held up the radio in one hand, while putting his finger to his lips with the other. Seemed they didn't trust the Americans anymore than she did.

They left the American radio far from Onyxhall's front doors, standing next to a rock with some of the men to listen for any call.

"Americans perfected the surveillance state," Pierrecin told the reconvened inhabitants beneath Onyxhall's blackened timbers. "Who knows how good that thing's ears are."

Candlelight lit the hall, everyone crowding for information on the new arrivals. Only the children were missing, watched by a few adults within the greenhouses of Perennial on the island far from the American ship. With the exception of those standing watch of their radio and two more their ship, all of Scuttle Star huddled once more within Onyxhall.

"You can't trust them," Isa said to Mahise and the other Mothers sitting at the long table. "Even I could see their lies. The one in the boat looked to be sizing up the spoils the entire time."

"I agree," Meyer said. "They didn't seem that friendly, despite the smiles."

"Why leave the radio, then?" someone in the audience asked.

"To listen, perhaps," Mother Mahise said with a shrug. "Or perhaps they really are here for a short visit."

This brought grumbling from the crowd upon which Isa pounced.

"You can't honestly believe that."

"You've spoken your piece," Mother Mahise said. "Let others—"

"No!" Isa stood. "You may have ran from the nightmare but it's found you. *We've* never known the outside world." She gestured to Sala and the others her age sitting on the floor. "Everything we have is on this island and they've come to take it. You know this and still you offer hope that maybe, *maybe* this time the Americans aren't out for blood."

"No one is saying that," Mother Mahise said, trying to calm the crowd's growing fear.

But Isa saw the nods her words elicited. Flush with energy from such attention, she barreled onward.

"We can't take that risk. If that ship is here it's here for one reason. To either burn all this or steal it. This crowded hall makes for a juicy target for all the bombs you told us the Americans love. How long 'til they realize such?"

She knew not from whence the words came. She hadn't prepared any sort of speech. But the mentioning of Onyxhall as a target struck a different kind of fear in the Mothers and the men. They recalled all too well American bombs.

"Alright," Mother Mahise said in a weary voice. "You've got it all figured out. What's your plan against an American warship, with its jets and helicopters? How do you propose we respond?"

What little enthusiasm she'd conjured evaporated with the question. "We have guns," she said in a tiny voice. Many in the room sneered or looked away.

"Against their warship?" Mahise asked. "Their attack helicopters?"

"Maybe nothing so complicated as all that." It was Meyer. He stroked his gray-flecked beard while looking toward the books lining the walls. "Why not invite them to dinner. If they haven't started bombing us already, maybe they're waiting. Let's use this time to get some of them here."

"And?" Mahise asked. "What then?"

He shrugged. "Feed them. Get 'em full and drunk. All smiles and refilled cups until they're nice and docile. Then, take some hostages. Gives us a bit of leverage at least. We can always decide later. Drown them in the sea. String them up from Arbor for all their friends to see."

Isa heard considerable mumbled agreement from the crowd.

"And if they decide to send their helicopters? Or their jets?" Mahise asked. "What then?"

"Perhaps," said Pierrecin, speaking as if his own plan was taking shape, "we might try sabotage. Get as many here to eat while we sneak aboard their ship."

"And how do you suggest we do that?" Mahise sounded desperate to dissuade the growing plans energizing the room.

"Yank every fuel line," Pierrecin said. "Cut every cable. And I'm no aircraft expert, but I'm fairly certain a few handfuls of rocks tossed within a jet turbine ruins any pilot's day."

Several of the men and even some Mothers voiced their agreement. Others volunteered. Crews of the old ships explained how easy damaging engines could be.

Others discussed how much liquor they had with which to get a group of American sailors drunk enough to piss themselves in their sleep. Isa let them feel how possible it was to defend their home before speaking. Offering encouragement that they truly possessed the sling and stone to topple the mighty Goliath slavering for all they'd built on Scuttle Star. She looked at Mahise.

Mahise looked old. Her dark skin seemed immune to wrinkles, but the years showed at the corners of her eyes as she weighed war. Isa loved her, as she did all the Mothers of Scuttle Star. But now was not the time for peace.

"Every moment only emboldens them further," Isa said. "Perhaps there was a reason no Americans came to Scuttle Star. Why none of the founders included a single one in their planning our refuge here. Well now they've come. And it up to us to keep them out."

Mahise turned to the other Mothers seated beside her. They nodded their assent.

"Very well," Mahise said. "Tomorrow night. We will prepare a feast." She nodded to Pierrecin. "*You* prepare your raid."

Bishop closed his eyes to fight the growing nausea, but it only seemed to worsen.

"How you doing Westy?" he called over the waves and the sputtering engine.

"Only the wheel is holding me up."

"Didn't say much to our new friends."

"Didn't wanna pass out and go into the drink. Not the impression the skipper ordered us to make."

Bishop had tried his damndest to look hale and hearty. Had smiled with confidence while giving what he'd hoped were firm handshakes. If years of aimlessly sailing the rising seas had taught them anything, it was that no one took in strays.

"You're doing fine," Bishop said in meager encouragement of the young petty-officer piloting the boat.

"I'm more concerned with how we get back aboard."

One more thing Bishop had put off thinking about. As they rounded their ship —the rusted, barnacle-encrusted, barely floating vessel once called *Reagan*—Bishop winced at the next obstacle awaiting them.

They tied the boat off to the thick cargo netting dangling from the aft section above the ship's massive screws. Like everything else aboard, the cranes used to lift the boats hadn't functioned in years. The two looked upwards for several minutes, swaying in the teal blue sea in dread of the three story climb to the hangar bay.

"You first," Bishop said. "I can always catch you if you fall."

"Neither of us could catch a cat," Weston said, beginning his climb. Bishop followed.

Each meter brought a longer rest, clutching the thick ropes as nausea, thirst, and hunger all vied against exhaustion to see which might loosen their grip and send them tumbling back into the sea. There was no point in calling for aid to those above. Not even an extended hand to help them the final few feet. Bishop and Weston had been sent ashore for one simple reason.

They were the only two with strength enough to go.

They reached the top after nearly twenty minutes climbing, rolling themselves over the rusted steel lip and falling to the hanger deck a few feet beneath. Bishop lay with his eyes closed, his heaving, raspy breaths alerting those within they'd returned. He heard them stirring about him.

"Had almost forgotten that smell," he said.

"One more thing to look forward to," Weston replied from beside him.

"What did they say?" a familiar voice spoke from nearby. Others joined it. Bishop opened his eyes and turned his head.

Commander Delgado had once been beautiful. Bishop remembered when he'd first met her, nearly eight years prior. Joining the Navy had probably saved his life. Between the crop failures and resulting food riots, being tucked aboard a carrier didn't seem a bad career path. Was hard to catch a bullet with several steel bulkheads surrounding you. And the food might not have been great, but the military had provided three hot, and more importantly, *regular* meals a day. In defiance of all logic, and in keeping with every crumbling society throughout history, those tasked with protection ate while the ones they were ostensibly protecting starved.

Delgado had been the ops-boss then. Bishop could still see that same woman hidden beneath the sunken cheeks, the blood-shot eyes and her stooped posture leaning heavily against a single crutch. She was all that was left of the command structure aboard *Reagan*.

"Will they have us?" she asked.

"Can't say." Bishop rose to a sitting position, his weakness abating some at the several hopeful stares turned his way from the numerous cots littering the hangar bay. "They seemed mighty curious about our aircraft. And why we were here and how many we were."

Delgado nodded while swaying, clinging to her crutch, eyes closed in concentration. "And how did they look?" she asked in a whisper.

It was Weston who answered. "Whole hell of a lot better than we do, Ma'am?"

"We gave them the radio," Bishop said. "Told them we'd like to come ashore for a bit before leaving. To stretch our legs and such. They haven't called, have they?" Bishop knew it was foolish to hope. But hope was all the starving, scurvy-stricken crew had left.

Delgado shook her head. "But the hard part's almost over. First rule of immigrating is *getting* there. Well, we're not quite there yet. But if we can get ashore, we'll at least have a shot of joining them. A shot at survival."

Bishop knew she wasn't just speaking to him, but to all those listening around them. Barely fifty souls remained of the thousands that had once crewed *Reagan*. In the far corner, Bishop looked to he bodies. The most recent to succumb. Once they'd sighted the fabled island, the one they'd spent long years seeking, they didn't dare return their shipmates to the sea lest they wash ashore. Hard to convince the locals you had something to offer when they found your friends sewed in shrouds. No one took in strays.

"Well," Delgado said, opening her eyes, "you both did well. We'll wait 'til morning and call them. Ask to send a few ashore, and see what they say. For now. Rest up."

Bishop got to his feet, and helped Weston to a cot before turning for his own. They could wait one more day. Most of them could, at least. Looking around, it was hard not to notice the ones who might not make it until then. Feeble breaths barely discernible as life. They might have another day. Would they have any more?

It was as Bishop reached his cot that they heard it. The sounds turning every head within the dim, echoing hangar. A radio crackling to life. Those with strength huddled around it. With desperate hopes they listened as Delgado conjured a confident voice and responded. As they listened, Bishop could feel the hope fill them, moving some to tears. An invitation from the island. A feast.

Bishop closed his eyes as several around him openly wept.

They were saved.

The plan may have been devious and treacherous, but Isa liked it. What she didn't like was being told to stay behind.

The mood was festive if subdued. Onyxhall was busy with preparations. They had a few occasions for feasts each year, but something so spontaneous was unheard of. The kitchens adjacent to the hall were overflowing with people stirring pots, kindling cookfires, and the constant coming and going of those bringing ingredients from the ships. Isa suspected such an elaborate feast might soothe the guilt at the night's coming treachery.

She'd pleaded with Pierrecin to allow her on the raid to the American ship.

"But I found it," she'd said as if that gave her some claim. "And I'm the oldest. I should be going along."

Pierrecin, indeed many of the other men, often treated her with more respect than the Mothers.

"You don't know the brutality of the Americans," he said. "The things they do in war. What they did to their own citizens within their borders." He looked away.

"I promise, you want no part of where we're going."

"But I can help."

"You'll be needed here. Now and in the future. Many of us may not return. If Scuttle Star is to survive, it needs women like you."

He would hear no more. She'd tried with the other men and handful of women going, but they defaulted to Pierrecin. She'd be stuck serving these idiots until they were drunk enough to be subdued. The plan wasn't violence unless called for. Several clubs, knives, and even a few rifles were hidden for when the time came.

"Hey. How's it going?" Sala's words woke her from her thoughts. She returned to chopping onions.

"Wonderful. Get to sit around and cook for a bunch of Americans who at any moment might start dropping bombs on us. Things are just *great*."

"I'm going on the raid," he said. She turned to look and saw he was looking at the floor. The same stooped posture as he hid his embarrassing overbite. She'd known him a long time. The two had spent a lot of time together being the nearest in age. It was all but assumed they'd eventually be partners. So caught up had she been in her murderous thoughts she hadn't considered anyone else.

"I didn't know," she said.

"I'm just helping with the canoes. Pierrecin says I'm not going aboard. I'm just supposed to signal a lookout on shore if anything goes wrong." He picked up an onion slice and popped it in his mouth. "It'll probably be fine," he said between crunching bites. "But I'd still rather stay here with you."

With a suddenness that was fast becoming common, a plan unfurled. She put down her knife.

"You going like that?" she said, running her fingers through his frizzy afro. He hadn't cut it in awhile.

He shrugged. "Just wear a cap, I guess."

She took his hand. "C'mon. I'll braid it for you. Let's get out of here."

They went to her room. It was built off Onyxhall as were all the other small bedrooms that offered a bit of privacy. She locked the door with the small wooden latch and the two sat on her bed.

"You haven't done my braids in forever."

"I know, right," she said, pulling his hair into thick strands while sitting behind him. It was tricky with the thin hempen string they had, but she'd learned how to wrangle his hair into braids long ago, and while not perfect, they always gave him a much different look. As the only two who'd once been teenagers together on the island, any new look was something appreciated.

"If this doesn't work . . ." he said trailing off. "Just get into the caves and hide. No matter how long it takes."

She had no intention of going into any caves.

"Wanna get high?" she asked.

"I probably shouldn't."

"I've got some in the drawer. Scored it from Mother Lang's good stuff in the hemp gardens the other day."

"I don't know. This isn't a game tonight. It's for real."

"You've got hours. But fine. Light it and pass it to me. If I'm going to be stuck here I'm getting high."

Sala grumbled but retrieved her little clay pipe and packed a bowl. Even from a meter away the stink of Mother Lang's herb tickled her senses. Isa took the pipe and leaned past him, bent to the candle on her nightstand, and took a pull.

She didn't cough, but came close. Mother Lang mostly grew the versatile hemp they used. But her other herb was potent enough to be just as valuable. Isa clouded the tiny room with her exhale, the candle light sending dancing shadows about the blackened timbers.

"Give me that," Sala said, relenting.

Isa smiled a wicked grin and passed him the pipe. They soon finished the bowl, the room reeking of their efforts. She pulled him back towards her from behind, and finished his braids.

How long had they done this? Been this close, this high, and never consummated things? Sure, they'd fooled around. As the only two of a similar age on the island, they'd messed with clumsy kisses and the most minor of petting. But with everyone on Scuttle Star so close, they'd felt like naughty cousins more than anything.

Both were certain of their mothers, but their fathers were another story. Still, the adults had assured them both they weren't any relation, and encouraged any relationship the two might explore.

Yet they never had. Only now, with the Americans lurking aboard their warship, and Isa plotting her next step, this might be their last chance.

"There," she said, pulling the hempen string tight on the final braid. "Finished." But she didn't let him go. And he didn't pull away. There were few words. The herb had excited them both to quiet action. They fumbled about for a bit, and it took awhile for them to intertwine, but once they did, the rhythm came naturally.

Isa was glad to have smoked. Through the pain, she even thought she saw the appeal of the not entirely unpleasant act. Lying on her back, embracing Sala above, she looked at her sand dollars.

The fifty or so strung through with hemp dangled in an arc from one corner of the ceiling to the other. It was then, her mind unfettered by the herb and looking at her little collection that she realized this might be her last night in her room, on Scuttle Star, or even alive.

They had to hit the Americans. Sabotage as much of their gear as possible while taking hostages. Scuttle Star was worth dying for. And, she realized, even worth killing for. She'd accepted that, but it was looking at her sand dollars when she felt the weight of what approached slithering about her.

She'd collected the sand dollars since she was a girl and had never been embarrassed about it. In all those years she'd never once found one whole. Always broken, she marveled at their natural symmetry. The seeming mathematical pattern radiating from their center. She'd wanted a single, complete specimen at the center of her little collection.

And, with them going to their likely death at the hands of the barbaric Americans, she'd never get that chance.

She squeezed Sala close when he finished, resisting his efforts to pull away.

"You sure?" he said, breathless after he finished.

She looked him in the eye and smiled before nodding. "I don't think it matters much after tonight, do you?"

He looked at her for a few heartbeats before nodding and rolling off her. "I guess not."

The two lay together in the candlelight for several silent minutes, their breathing slowing while the sweat dried from their bodies. Isa waited.

It didn't take long. The past few days, first with the storm, then with the arrival of the Americans, had meant little rest for either of them. That, coupled with the herb and their exertions, Sala was soon sleeping beside her.

She untangled herself from him and looked at her long-time friend. She felt the slightest guilt. Sala always passed out like clockwork after smoking. As tired as the entire island was, she knew the weed would do the trick. She dressed quietly, snuffed the candle, and climbed out the window.

The shadows were long from the palms crowding close to Onyxhall. Above, their boughs glowed golden in the sun's slanting rays. Within, the bustle of the feast preparations continued, but outside, Isa had the white sands to herself.

She hurried towards Sala's room and crept in through his window. On his bed, in the dim evening light, she was pleased to see he'd set out his gear for the raid. His clothes fit well enough, but she was glad to have her own worn, yet sturdy boots. She dressed in his patched coveralls, surplus brought in the exodus to Scuttle Star. She tucked her short hair into his cap, and pulled it low. She was pleased to see he'd left a hempen cloth used as a sort of bandanna. She tied this about her face, leaving only her eyes peeking from the cap's brim. The disguise wouldn't withstand the daylight, but in the dark, she might just pull it off. She tucked Sala's knife into her boot and left the way she'd came.

The canoes were kept near Gourd, the two beached ships where they grew their many pumpkins and squashes. Only a sliver of purple twilight lit the tip of the horizon, and several stars glowed to life above.

"Sala?" Pierrecin's deep voice called as she approached.

Isa swallowed her fear, her heart thumping, and slouched.

A lifetime together with Sala had given her ample time to observe his gestures. As children, she'd mocked the way he hid his massive overbite with cruel impressions. It was effortless to produce the same stance now. She grunted in what she hoped was a good approximation of his voice.

"You're in the back," Pierrecin said, striding past without a second look toward the last canoe in the line. "Keep them all together. And if things go wrong, signal the shore." He pulled a small clay lantern from the canoe. "It's already lit," he said, sliding the wooden slat to reveal the light within. "Keep it dark. But if we hit trouble, flash the shore. Mother Carter will be watching." He waved the lantern to the bridge of the nearest ship and was soon greeted by another lantern waving its acknowledgment.

"OK," she grunted once more, praying not to arouse suspicion.

Pierrecin put his hands on her shoulders. "Don't be afraid, son," he said as she once more looked away. "Whatever happens, stay with the canoes. If we're not back, paddle home and get to the caves." With a final squeeze, he returned to his preps with the others.

She'd done it! The feeling was electric. Isa lurked about the rear, away from the others.

It was time. The herb lingered, calming her excitement while steeling her to what approached. The Americans had come to steal everything from them. No different from when their barbaric nation had chained its first slave and slaughtered its last native. Ceaseless murder and war now brought to Isa's own shores. A similar offense was now Scuttle Star's *only* defense. And win, lose, or draw, Isa was more than happy to die taking as many of the murderers with her as possible.

Mahise had considered herself prepared for the Americans. Being from Kenya, she'd seen their work over the years in neighboring nations. The disastrous interventions. The support for the most corrupt. The endless bombing campaigns. She'd steeled herself for hulking warriors with ravening gazes surveying their future spoils.

At seeing what wastrel creatures had instead shambled ashore, not even Mahise could hide her shock.

"They look half-dead," Meyer had whispered as they approached Onyxhall. "And closer to dead than the other half."

How they'd managed the three hundred meters from the shore she still wasn't sure. Pale, gaunt faces with sunken cheeks and fine uniforms clinging to skeletal arms, they looked more shade than soldier.

Anticipating danger, they'd stocked the long tables with pitchers of wine and surplus bottles with the whiskey and gin they fermented on the island. Beside these were wooden bowls heaped with potato salad, fresh peaches, oranges and other citrus, bowls of green curry, crab they'd pulled from the pots that morning, as well as boiled eggs from their hens. The plan to get the Americans fat, drunk and content before falling upon them now seemed silly with their pathetic victims before them. Mahise could have throttled them all with her bare hands.

"Go slow," the one called Bishop told the others as they feebly scooped food.

"Wine," one woman said, sniffing her cup before taking a drink.

"Doc didn't say nothing about wine," another cautioned her. "I don't know if we should."

"Fuck that." She took a long drink.

The others dove in as well, starting with nibbles but relishing each bite as they sampled each dish. Mahise looked to the others from Scuttle Star who were as bewildered as she. The two groups spoke, idle conversation as the Americans ate, but the silences grew longer until one woman, face ashen, began to sway.

"I think I need some air," she said, attempting to stand. She would have gone face first into the potato salad if Bishop hadn't attempted to catch her. Unfortunately he was little better and the two looked about to fall together until Mother Lang rushed to catch them both.

"You too need— my god," she said, stunned. "Mahise get over here."

She reached them in three quick strides, gasping as she took the woman in her arms.

"We're fine," the woman said with tears in her eyes. "Please, don't send us away."

Mahise had spent years reforesting the areas surrounding Nairobi—until local politicians flush with Chinese bribes bulldozed their efforts for high-rises. During that time she'd encountered starvation. Shantytowns scratching the most meager of existence against the city. The founders' mysterious summons to board a ship and sail from the collapsing world had felt angelic, especially after watching their hard work ripped from the earth and replaced with concrete. Holding the wasted girl, she was reminded all too suddenly of the world they'd tried to forget.

"Hush," Mahise said, kneeling to the floor with the girl in her arms. "Lay him down as well, Lang." She may not have been comfortable planning a kidnapping and ransom, but as a Mother of Scuttle Star, she knew how to help. The orders came quick. Calling on other Mothers and men by name with explicit commands.

"Move the tables against the bookshelves. Bring the tatami cushions and lay them all down. First-aid kits, bring them all."

The other Americans protested but were soon lying on the makeshift litters in the cleared space. The relic medical gear, all they had that didn't require batteries, were soon brought from deep within the caves where it was kept safe from the devouring humidity and elements.

Mahise plugged her ears with a stethoscope, and slid the other end beneath the woman's uniform top.

"How long since you've eaten?" she asked, eyes wide at what she felt beneath the woman's shirt.

"Weeks?" She offered a tiny shrug.

Each rib poked through parchment-thin flesh. The baggy tunic had hid her distended belly. Quick consultation revealed the others were no better. Mahise continued her commands.

"Heat the rice. Mix it with milk." She looked to the girl in her arms. Hair that appeared simply blonde beneath the warm glow of the lamps looked translucent against Mahise's dark skin. Brittle and thin, strands fell away from the slightest touch.

"Why did you come?" Mahise asked in disbelief. "Surely there were others aboard in better health."

Bishop laughed a weak chuckle. "We were the only ones strong enough to make the trip."

"Why not tell us your condition?" Mahise asked. "Why the lies?"

"No one takes in strays," he said. "Not anymore. You bring something to offer. Or you're sent away to die."

"Please don't send us away," the girl in Mahise's arms pleaded. "We just need food. We can work, all of us." This brought mumbled confirmations from her companions.

Mahise closed her eyes. All they'd built on Scuttle Star. The bountiful, well-tended gardens, always providing more than enough to dry and store, and they'd hoarded it as greedily as those in the world they'd fled. How quick they'd been to judge the Americans. And it was they who'd acted so like that fallen nation.

"No one's going anywhere," Mahise said, wiping a tear from the young woman's eye.

"The others," she said, her eyes closed as exhaustion overtook her. "They're worse than us. Please. You must go to them."

"Yes, we . . ." Mahise looked to Lang, the two remembering at once the other half to their scheme.

"Oh hell," the British woman said.

"Get the radio," Mahise said. "Ring the bell. And hurry!"

‡‡

They discovered Isa aboard the ship.

"Where's Sala?" Pierrecin demanded in an angry whisper. The raiding party crouched on an outside walkway ringing the hangar bay beneath the flight deck. A moonless night left the massive spray of stars their only illumination.

"Safe," she said. "Let's go."

Pierrecin grabbed her arm. "This isn't a game," he hissed.

She shook herself free from his grip and snapped Sala's blade from her boot. "I know."

Shaking his head, he moved off, the rest of the group following. Little of the starlight penetrated the hangar's dark. The occasional cough met their ears but they saw nothing of the Americans' arsenal. Arriving at a metal stairwell, they ascended to the flight deck.

They'd expected sentries. Someone watching over their aircraft. Isa's hand continually wandered to the knife in her boot for the first fool crossing their path.

They found nothing. The Milky Way arced over the sprawling flight deck, the only other light mere pinpricks from Scuttle Star in the distance. Against the stars, they saw their two targets.

"Hurry," Pierrecin said. "We deal with these, then the hangar."

Isa would settle for a little sabotage before the real fun began. It was unlikely they could neutralize everyone, so ensuring their planes remained on the ground was vital. She hurried to the helicopter with one half of the group while the other went for the jet. She leapt upon the helo, clambering onto the top beneath the main rotor, eager to gut the engine of every hose and cable.

It didn't take long.

"The hell?" someone whispered from below.

The single line Isa found crumbled into salt-corroded dust the moment she jerked it free. The rest of the rotor apparatus was a similar ruin. She slid down the side and rejoined the others.

"The whole cockpit is gutted," Mother Mansour said. "The only flying this thing will do is over the side when it's pushed."

They moved to the jet and found a similar discussion. Fuselage panels had been pried free only to reveal gaping holes missing entire components. They made sure to toss handful of rocks within its turbine, but the plane looked as airworthy as the relic helicopter.

"The rest must be below," Isa said, hurrying back toward the stairwell before any could protest.

They crept down toward the hangar, as dark as the caves beneath Mount Solemn. With their lanterns shuttered, the darkness was impenetrable. And while their eyes might be worthless, their noses worked just fine.

"Stop," Pierrecin whispered.

Death. The fetid stench of it hung about the place the further within they crept. Was this some sort of plague ship? The Americans' version of disease ridden blankets to weaken their enemies? Nothing was out of the realm of Isa's suspicions when it came to the Americans, but her doubts at the junked aircraft continued to grow.

"What are you doing here?"

The group turned at the rasping voice. Silhouetted against the starlight, leaning heavily on a crutch, was a woman.

Isa lunged. She fumbled her knife free and pressed it to the woman's throat while grabbing the collar of her tattered coveralls.

"Isa, stop!" Pierrecin wasn't whispering anymore. His deep voice echoed about the cavernous darkness.

"Please," the woman pleaded.

"You won't take it," Isa hissed in the woman's ear. "This is our island." This was a warship. Americans didn't arrive to one's shores to make friends. If the others refused to act, then *she* would. She pressed the blade further toward the woman's scrawny neck, hands trembling as she fought down vomit.

"Put down the knife, Isa," Pierrecin said. "Can't you see? These people need our help."

Isa was no stranger to knife work. Shucking clams, notching wood, a hundred other daily tasks on Scuttle Star gave her some confidence. It wouldn't take much to end the starveling woman in her grasp.

She needn't have bothered. The woman simply collapsed, going limp until she slid free and fell to a heap on the deckplates.

"Leave her alone," a voice called from the darkness. Other voices joined it as Isa turned, her knife still shaking. Pierrecin and the others opened their lanterns. The light within was weak, but in that darkness, they might have well been torches. Isa's knife clattered to the deck.

There were cots. Hundreds vanishing into the darkness. Upon each were corpses in rags. The few that moved waved skeletal hands while pleading to leave their skipper be. A few rose, shambling toward the light, hands like claws outstretched in whatever threat they could muster.

"Don't hurt her," one woman said, moving closer. "Please." She stood for a moment before falling forward, the exertion proving too much.

Pierrecin rushed to catch her, cradling the woman in his arms as he knelt to the deck, lying her down with care.

Pierrecin stood, stepped toward the Americans, and spoke, his Hatian accent so familiar to Isa.

"We can help," he said. "We had no idea how bad things were. We have water. And can bring food." He turned to Isa and the others. "Help them back to their cots. Give them all the water we have. We need numbers. How many. In what condition. Hurry."

He might have well been Mother Mahise the way he took charge. They moved among the Americans, offering sips from their canteens while giving quiet words of aid. They had food. Medical staff. It was all on the island, and they'd soon bring more. Watching her friends, hearing the tearful thanks from the dying, Isa moved to join them.

"Not you," Pierrecin said. "Help me with her." They knelt to the woman Isa had nearly killed. She stirred to life as they dripped water from a canteen onto her cracked lips.

"Thank you," she managed as she mustered the power to sip the canteen.

"What happened here?" Pierrecin asked. "Why didn't you tell us you needed help?"

The woman managed a smile. "No one takes in strays. Not anymore. You bring something to offer. Or you're sent away." She looked at Isa. "This was more the welcome we expected."

Isa turned from the woman's gaze. Left her to Pierrecin before hurrying to the rail at the hangar's edge.

The sea was quiet beneath, silent like the endless spray of stars above. She didn't want the others to see her tears. As the oldest born on Scuttle Star, she often felt like a child. Even after what she'd shared with Sala, she felt like one now.

She'd expected to die. To go forth against a terrible foe and fight to protect what was theirs. Seeing them in their desperation, crying at a few drinks of clear, fresh water, Isa realized how childish her dreams of some glorious death had been.

Wiping away her tears, a new sound shattered the darkness. Clear and crisp it sounded across the waves. It's sound a reminder of all they'd built. Scuttle Star's mighty bell comforted her from across the sea. A radio soon squawked to life, and Isa smiled in the dark. It was Mother Mahise.

Mahise arrived with the dawn, her canoe carrying bowls of porridge wrapped in banana leaves and tied with hempen string. Alongside were baskets of citrus and canteens of water. Others from the island joined her, their many canoes secured to the cargo net dangling to the sea beneath the hangar.

"That's enough for now," Mahise said, taking the bowl of porridge from Commander Delgado. "We need to go slow." She handed her a lemon slice. "Suck on this."

Isa watched the woman accept the slice before lying back on the cot. Beneath the sunken cheeks Isa could discern her previous beauty. Indeed, some of it seemed to have returned already. While the daylight had revealed several corpses among the starving, the islanders were seeing to the living.

"Are more of you coming?" Isa asked.

"Quiet," Mahise said. "There's time for that later."

"It's OK," Delgado said, her eyes still closed. "There are no others. Finding this place was our last chance."

"You knew about Scuttle Star?" Isa pressed on.

"Not the name. But these places have been a myth for years."

"These . . . *places*?" Mahise asked, her own curiosity piqued.

Delgado smiled before answering. "You don't think you're the only one do you?" She opened her eyes. "We'd been on the lookout for years. Intel had mentioned reports of surplus bulk-container ships being purchased. Loaded with dirt and sent off god knows where. That was back when the world had *intel*. Or satellites even."

"Satellites," Mahise said, looking away.

"I wouldn't worry," Delgado said. She went on to explain the endless wars, each battle fiercer and more pointless than the last as resources dwindled. "By the end, they sent us and the few remaining ships into the South China Sea without even bullets or bombs. We were ordered to ram Chinese ships if possible." She scoffed. "By that point, what few of our squadron remained simply fled, flying away forever. To where, who knows. Why whatever brass remained stateside thought starving sailors would fight is beyond me. The last of us struck out for this place."

She fought to a sitting position despite Mahise's admonitions.

"There are no others, girl," she said, staring hard at Isa. "Between the crop failures, the droughts, and the floods, society—what remains of it—is scaling back to something a lot less complicated. I wouldn't expect any others ever on your shores."

She lay back down, the exertion enough that she soon nodded off to sleep. Mahise checked her heart-rate once more before leading Isa toward the rail of the ship facing the island. The sea beneath was deep blue so far from Scuttle Star's shores. The lazy, rolling waves looked glossy without the foam nearer the island. Arbor's bushy boughs were bright in the late morning sun. A sea of lush green above the rusted hulk of the beached ship. Vineyard looked orderly with its rows of grapes beside Arbor's leaves. Mount Solemn stood sentinel above it all.

"I haven't seen the island from this far in a long time," Mahise said.

"I don't trust them," Isa said.

"I do."

"Why? How do you know there's not more on the way as we speak?"

"Because I've been hungry. And frightened. Just like them." She turned and looked at Isa. "And you never have."

Isa made to speak but Mahise hushed her with a raised hand.

"I recognize your fire. It comes from the women in our family." She chuckled. "I wish you could have met your grandmother. My father stood a head taller than her but she could cow that man with a single word." She was silent a few moments more, the distant roar of the crashing waves onshore filling the silence. "I wish you could have met them both. But this island is all you've known. A full belly. Clean air. Quiet nights without gunfire. You know our abundance. We have enough to share."

"If Americans are so innocent, then why did the founders not include a single one when they sent you to this place?"

Her mother didn't have an answer for that. Isa couldn't remember the last time she'd had a moment alone with her mother. As de-facto leader of Scuttle Star, there always seemed someone pressing for her time.

"There's something . . . Sala and I—"

"It was wrong what you did to him," Mahise said. "Tricking him like that and coming here. You embarrassed him and I want you to apologize."

She'd wanted to discuss what they'd shared. That she was now a woman, and Sala a man. So much had happened the previous night, she'd been glad for a moment to unload the burden. Explore it with her mother.

And she'd lectured her like a child instead.

"I'm going back," Isa said. She was tired of this plague ship full of liars. Of her blind elders eating up their sob stories. They'd flock to shore soon enough. She wanted to enjoy unspoiled Scuttle Star for what little time remained.

The ride back was soothing, the waves gentle as she kept far enough from shore before they touched bottom and grew teeth. She paddled around toward Herbal and Legume, the ships on the lee of the island where the approach was more gentle. Each beached ship bursting with their crops was its own oasis. Despite her weariness, the nearly hour-long journey soothed some of the night's tension. She looked forward to the cool quiet of her room.

She winced when she saw the man on the beach, leaning heavily on a stick.

"Heya," he said, his dopey smile as bright as the day he'd first arrived. "We meet again."

She dragged her canoe onto the beach, beneath the swaying palms far from the surf. Legume rocked behind her, steel shrieking as it swayed.

"Shouldn't you be in bed or something?" she said, moving past Bishop.

"They tried to keep me there. But I needed some air. This place is amazing. Wanted to get a look at it. Maybe you could show me around. What kind of name is Scuttle Star, anyway?"

She shrugged. "From above, all the ships surrounding the island look like a starfish."

The idea came to her with a wickedness to which she was becoming accustomed. They were alone. Who would know? She turned, biting her lower lip with both hands behind her back.

"If you wanna see, I know a place," she said. "Little up the mountain. You can see everything." She stepped close to him, with a demure yet naughty expression. "Thing is, nobody can see *us*. What do you say? How good are you feeling?" She dragged a finger down his chest.

"Whole lot better now."

There was indeed a small lookout. A little cliff her and Sala frequented. And beneath the edge, an easy twenty meter drop. It wouldn't be hard to get him up there. He was already eager for her. And when they got there— oops, guess he stepped too close to the edge. She'd warned the fool not to follow her. But he'd insisted. And, if for some reason the fall didn't finish him, she was confident a rock existed that could be dropped on his head.

She strode past him, growing more comfortable with the murderous plots that came so quickly since discovering the Americans.

"You coming?" she asked, turning toward him with a playful look.

And that was when she saw it. So perfect was it resting on the sand that she gaped, her mouth hanging open like a fool. She'd walked right past it. A flawless circle undamaged by the waves. Oblong gaps at each point of the central star. She'd have to restring her entire collection to add this to the center, but the effort would be worth it. Gone were any thoughts but the sheer joy stretching back to years of fruitless searching. After all these years, she'd finally found her perfect sand dollar.

Then there was the American.

"The hell?" he said, looking down at the crunching sound beneath his boot. "Oh. Just a seashell. So." He flashed her an idiot grin. "Where we headed?"

She moved toward him, and knelt down, hoping that perhaps it hadn't shattered. That some part had survived. She slid her hand beneath, and watched it crumble to dust.

She grimaced, closing her eyes while the American babbled on. Something snapped inside her. The combined stress of the upturned little island and a sleepless, stressful night. What had she been thinking? What would Mahise, or the others, think of her? Was she really so eager to bloody her hands? To avenge some as-yet-uncommitted crime?

Isa was tired. She stood, looked out at the beached ships surrounding them, and turned toward Onyxhall.

"Come," she hissed before storming off.

He offered further protests, wondering about her previous plans before following with cries to wait. She didn't look back, but trudged toward Onyxhall on weary legs that threatened to fail her at each step.

The Americans remained within, as did the remnants of the feast. What might spoil had been eaten or carted to the caves while the fruits and juices remained. The Americans looked positively resurrected from the near corpses she'd seen on their ship. She knew a night's rest and a single full belly hadn't achieved such miracles.

It was simply hope. Hope for a future. Hope for something more than starving to death at sea.

"This way," she commanded when he rejoined her. Not looking back as she went to her room.

"Thought you were hoping for some privacy," he said, breathing heavily and leaning upon the blackened timbers of her door frame. "But I guess this works."

She stared hard at him, seeing if he'd understand. It took him a few moments as his eyes wandered her tiny dwelling, but his gaze finally rested on the collection of broken sand dollars strung in twin arcs over her bed.

"You collect those?"

"Yes. And I never, in my twenty-four years, found a whole one. Until a few minutes ago."

Realization washed the smile from his face. "And I stepped on it."

They stood like that for several moments before he again spoke.

"Look. We're here to work. Same as anyone here. We're not pirates or freeloaders. Once we're well, we'll be at the chores like all of you."

She sighed, thinking of the broken sand dollar. While still galling, such concerns felt ridiculously childish. As childish as her foolish heroics the night before.

Or an imagined plan of murder.

"Get some rest." She moved to the door, and as he stepped from the threshold, she shut it tight.

Isa had no sooner lay down and closed her eyes when she heard the knock. She stormed to the door to tell the moron to go away. Instead, when she opened it, she saw Sala.

"Can I come in?"

He looked different. He was standing up straight and not attempting to hide his overbite. His hair remained braided from the night before. Just the way she liked it.

"Yeah." She let him in, locking the door behind them.

"Made me look pretty stupid last night."

She lay back down, closing her eyes and wondering if she'd ever be allowed to sleep.

"Did you get in trouble?" she asked.

"Did you?"

They compared stories of the previous night, Sala eager to hear of what she'd seen and her just as interested in what the visiting Americans had been like. After a few moments, he lay down beside her.

"So what now?" he asked.

"They get well. Then they get to work. Same as us."

"I *meant* us," he said, running a finger down her cheek.

"Oh." So much had happened in the previous days. With Sala, she discovered another shame in her dishonest seduction of the American. Now she would have to deal with that as the fool likely thought her sincere. She decided to stop thinking and simply curled into Sala, burying her head in his chest. She felt happy with him, and found the weariness melting away as comfortable sleep overtook her.

"I didn't sleep all night," she mumbled.

Sala pulled away from her and stood. "Don't sleep too much. It's Monday. You're on compost."

She rolled onto her back and groaned at thoughts of sifting for soldierfly larvae to feed the hens picking through the islanders' waste.

"Thanks for reminding me."

"That's what I'm here for." He leaned down and kissed her. As tired as she was, she kissed back and wondered if there was time for more, but he pulled away.

"Get some sleep. I'll bring you some lunch later. Best thing about a feast is the leftovers."

He left, and she fell into sleep within moments.

Deciding what to do with the Americans had been simple. Deciding what to do with their ship had been something else. The Americans insisted upon its utility. That the nuclear power-plant was safe and could even be rigged to provide electricity to the island. While some on Scuttle Star pondered this idea, Mahise vetoed it immediately.

"The founders didn't send us here to recreate the world we fled," she told them in crowded Onyxhall some weeks after their arrival. The island and its bounty had done them wonders. They were lean but strong. Tanned and hale from days of full bellies and work about Scuttle Stars' many gardens, arbors and vineyards.

In the end, it was decided to deal with the ship the way they knew best. After being stripped of everything of value, it would be sailed to the deepest ocean within range of their canoes, and with the assistance of the islanders, scuttled. Its nuclear core sent to the bottom where it was hoped it could dissipate harmlessly.

Isa sat with Sala on the bluffs above the island, on the small shelf beneath Mount Solemn where she'd once plotted murder. They watched the mammoth carrier sail into the twilight.

"You still mad they wouldn't let you go?" Sala asked.

She'd wanted to help send it to the bottom. But the work would be perilous, as would the canoe trip back. She might have fought harder for it if not for what she'd learned a few days prior. She'd not yet told Sala she was late. Her mom had cautioned her against telling too many people so early.

"Nothing's worse than having to explain a miscarriage after a joyful announcement," Mahise had told her. "No less to the father. Give it a couple months before you let people know."

"Not really," she said, leaning her head on Sala's shoulder. "I'd been to that ship once. Maybe once was enough."

THE FLIGHT PATH

BY ALISTAIR HERBERT

THE TREE GROWS. It falls, dying, at the Darkwards edge of the flat, and a small bird shoots out and under from the falling branches; they see it flitting and dodging because the tree's howling crack calls them out of their game. The bird is a tree sparrow; the tree is an arrow-straight, over-tall pine. It comes down too quick and too slow; it rests halfway against a neighbour and slides again, dead and living branches flicking each other away like tinder sticks. Reddish moss clings to the trunk and spiders prepare to make another adjustment. The thing returns to the warring ground, and mother dirt eats.

It lands and they turn reluctantly back to the game, not hearing the low murmurs beyond the branches, but a little more aware of their own blood. They're all approaching young adulthood except one: Ela, who follows her sister up to the flat because her sister doesn't refuse her. Her name means "from elsewhere" and she stands small, hovering at the edge of the game with her weight on one foot, the other nervily shuggling the crumble floor.

Autumn is turning to winter and the breeze is rising, but the clouds keep them warm. They come here to play because it feels a long way from home, and because some of their parents call it dangerous. There are trees on two sides, sheer cliff on another, and behind them the steep path back down to Glimmer.

The girl in the middle wears a blindfold and spins in place. The others move counter around her in a loose ring and listen to her chant.

The wheel turns, and mother burns; the wheel turns, and mother burns.

She gains pace and the noise in the trees can't compete with the thrill of the game. The children join hands or bump shoulders. Ela slips into the circle because she can't stand apart from it, and some of them smile about her—they're all alert.

The blind girl's arm flies up and she points and shouts three times in three directions.

Die in a fire. Die in a fire. Die in a fire.

If the girl singles you out, you drop to the ground. Drop too slow and you forfeit. The others howl in delight as her second victim fails—a short, dark boy who licks his lips too often. He drops anyway in confusion but they howl him back up to stand out the rest of the game in his place. The winner chooses his forfeit; the circle narrows without him.

The clouds tower and the trees talk to each other about the other noise. It feels like evening but it's not; cats and small creatures scurry with wide open eyes and everyone feels a little strange. Possibilities creep back in from the bristling thicket and you start to believe the stories because they're real: the wild world is the world. The wind is rising.

The blind girl points without shouting but her target doesn't fall for the trick; the dance continues. The circle quickly tightens to two survivors and the others watch. There's nothing special about surviving—it's the blind girl's random choice —but they feel special anyway and they join hands, laughing and stumbling, making it harder for themselves to circle the girl. Her lip curls and she chooses how to make her bet: if she grabs one of them she wins; if she misses she shares the losers' forfeit. The last boy pulls faces and bumps around on purpose, encouraging the little girl whose hands he's holding to laugh.

This is where the game turns ugly, if it turns ugly; the rules change, or a fight breaks out, and the crowd are as likely to cheer as to call it unfair. They're fickle and there are many paths to the thing they really want from the game: the truth of the world laid bare, a glimpse of the simple natural laws they instinctively know lurk behind the more confusing rules which their parents insist they learn and follow.

It happens quickly but Ela sees the arms coming for her. The blind girl aims her lunge well; she looks for a way out but finds nothing. She can only accept the gamble; she wants to play so she plays, and the blind girl catches her; no parent is coming to save her, no sister can protect her; she steps into the game by her own will. Her search for an escape complicates the situation, but really it's cruelly and beautifully simple. One bad dodge and the rules say she must concede.

The pointer feels her hands close on fabric and snag victorious in the folds. She smiles but she hears the kid cry out, the boy laughing behind her, and she realises her victim is Ela, the little one who's not really her friend, and her grip slackens slightly in uncertainty. It's unsporting to prey on smaller children, but here her hesitation costs her the game: the child twists and scrapes and breaks free, cheating, and she lifts her blindfold to see everyone laughing at her, and the young girl weeping and running on wobbling feet for the trees. She curses and she doesn't want to laugh and shrug it off, as she must in order to rejoin them in good standing. She can't handle unfairness.

Ela runs and cries without quite knowing why. She knows the older children now see her as the girl who cries at games, and the shame of that feeling is bigger than her body can hold. She runs for the hill path and quickly passes the trees and comes up into the last light. She wants to die. She doesn't want to die: she wants the pointer not to catch her.

She feels the breeze of evening banish the day. She hears the low murmur of noise become a roar, but there's nothing to see. The noise echoes across the sky and bounces off hills and trees. She pays it no mind; to hold onto fears, they all say, is to die in a box you make for yourself. On the hill the air fills ears and billows through clothes, and it's impossible to anticipate the hiding places of wolves, thugs, freezing clouds—so you come or you don't. She sees small birds play above their nests in the heather, flying against the wind and hovering in place, as if hanging from string. The wind is in the feathers, the old sheep's cleverness bending the wind arch, everything working together to place the bird. She can't put any of this into words, but she feels it and wants it for herself. Her own life is a struggle to exert mastery, not to more sensibly align, but she doesn't know it.

On the flat the other children are seeing the dragon. It drops from the sky with a crackling roar cutting clouds and shaking the trees; it spits smoke and fills the narrow space above them with noise and confusion.

They panic: some freeze, some run for cover, some pray to the sun god to protect them. The dragon passes overhead with a stripe of smoke in its wake, and it doesn't seem to see them. It disappears; the noise drops; the smoke dissipates, harmless as dandelion seeds; and the children doubt their own eyes and ears, but they cower anyway, full of trauma and exhilaration. The game provides the same feeling in smaller mouthfuls, and the dragon's bigness overwhelms them. Its shape is too hard to understand, not the sparrow's shape of life or the spidery, crow-like shape of death which they know well enough, but utterly smooth, the shape of no-life, of no place for life. They all only want to be out of its way.

On the hill Ela watches a crow rise and turn with the wind, letting the air sweep it sideways and back such that it spans a mile or more of the valley in one arcing movement. The grey-green land it crosses is immortal and asleep. She can't go back down to meet the others. She imagines them leaving, her sister dutifully waiting, neither of them wearing clothes for a night of winter rain. She knows she needs to move but she struggles all the same. The shame weighs heavy on her.

It's right that she should want to change her life. Children know this; most young adults forget it. Something is calling her which she can only learn if no tall people are watching. Below her the others are running home, and fear of dragons is spreading—into Glimmer, the town, and from there out again to the hamlets.

Alone, she vows to the new rain and the trees, vows to the watching moon, to run from nothing: in the growing gloom she changes herself. The oath is a point of light, a tool she must use, no matter its suitability, to chart clear and simple lines through unmet clouds.

A small bat or a big moth flits near her face without her seeing, and she looks back at the trees. It occurs to her that she is neither child nor woman nor inbetween, but a wild creature wetting her face alongside all the others in the endless dance of the world. The pride she treasures, the home she loves, the bravery she invents are all only a girl pretending she's not the animal with wide eyes she knows she is.

But then, of course, aren't we all only wild creatures pretending?

A storm is visible, gathering over the hill; the moon hides. Day turns into night. The wheel turns and the mother burns. The rain begins.

DON'T MISS A SINGLE ISSUE OF INTO THE RUINS

Already a subscriber?

Renew Today

Visit intotheruins.com/renew
or send a check for $39 made out to Figuration Press to
the address below

*Don't forget to include the name and address attached to your
current subscription and to note that your check is for a renewal.
Your subscription will be extended for four more issues.*

Not yet a subscriber?

Subscribe Today

Visit intotheruins.com/subscribe
or send a check made out to Figuration Press for $39 to:

Figuration Press
3515 SE Clinton Street
Portland, OR 97202

*Don't forget to include your name and mailing address,
as well as which issue you would like to start with.*

Made in the
USA
Lexington, KY